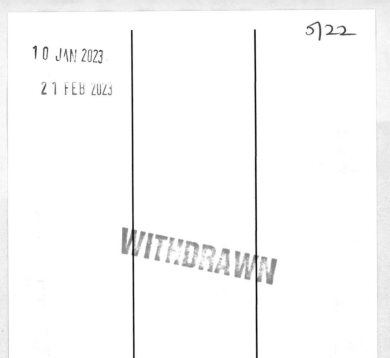
Literary Review

'This is a doc... authentic feel of a race ag... to miss it'

A FINE
MADNESS

A FINE
MADNESS

A novel inspired by the life and
death of Christopher Marlowe

ALAN JUDD

**SIMON &
SCHUSTER**

London · New York · Sydney · Toronto · New Delhi

First published in Great Britain by Simon & Schuster UK Ltd, 2021
This paperback edition published 2022

1 3 5 7 9 10 8 6 4 2

Simon & Schuster UK Ltd
1st Floor
222 Gray's Inn Road
London WC1X 8HB

Simon & Schuster Australia, Sydney
Simon & Schuster India, New Delhi

www.simonandschuster.co.uk
www.simonandschuster.com.au
www.simonandschuster.co.in

A CIP catalogue record for this book
is available from the British Library

Paperback ISBN: 978-1-4711-8024-8
eBook ISBN: 978-1-4711-8023-1
Audio ISBN: 978-1-4711-8162-7

Typeset in Palatino by M Rules
Printed and bound by CPI Group (UK) Ltd, Croydon, CR0 4YY

To Kate, with thanks

Neat *Marlow* bathed in the *Thespian* springs
Had in him those braue translunary things,
That the first Poets had, his raptures were,
All ayre, and fire, which made his verses cleere,
For that fine madnes still he did retaine,
Which rightly should possesse a Poets braine.

MICHAEL DRAYTON,
'Of Poets & Poesie'

HISTORICAL NOTE

This novel draws on historical characters and events, principally on records of the death of Christopher Marlowe, on records of Sir Francis Walsingham's secret service and on the life of Thomas Phelippes, Walsingham's gifted decipherer. So far as is known, Phelippes and Marlowe never met; their relationship as described here and all the interactions between them are invented. The interrogation of Phelippes and the postscript are also invented, although much of what he describes happened and most of the people he mentions existed. There is no record of Marlowe having been involved in secret service to the extent portrayed, although there is documentary evidence and evidence by association that he engaged in some sort of confidential government work. Incidents such as fights he was involved in, his attempted coining and remarks made about him by contemporaries are, however, mostly based on record.

Authoritative and comprehensive accounts of the world of the Elizabethan secret service and of Marlowe himself may be found in Stephen Alford's *The Watchers* and Charles Nicholl's *The Reckoning*.

CHAPTER ONE

Very well, sir, I hereby solemnly promise that I, Thomas
Phelippes, under oath, will tell all I know of the man.

But he has been dead these thirty years and I cannot be
far from my own end. Nor is my memory what it was. And
I am still amazed, sir, that you come to my cell with ale and
provisions and kind words, saying that the King, King James
himself, commands that I tell you all I knew of him, everything.
Yet you do not tell me why His Majesty enquires after a forgotten poet and play-maker. Almost forgotten. I do not know what
he wants to know. All I can offer is whatever scraps of memory
are left and pray they will be fit for the royal table.

However, I am grateful, sir, for what you bring and for
your company. Hearing yesterday of the Court's interest in
me prompted the governor here to move me to these more
comfortable quarters, with more coals and candles, as you
see, as well as fresh paper, quills and ink. Which is no less
than I need anyway when I have to labour at work which the
government that imprisons me still demands. God knows
how it pains my head and wearies my sight, yet I confess it

gives some pleasure. My only pleasure here. Along with my wife, Mary – whom God preserve – mathematic has ever been my love, you see. Although I no longer decipher with that swift facility I once commanded, it is still my delight to puzzle out men's hidden meanings.

Yet I cannot promise to decipher Christopher Marlowe for you. He was a man I knew only in part. He never opened his heart to me, nor perhaps to any, but I now think he may have shown more of it than I had eyes to see or ears to hear in those days of our youth. Although often in company and with wide acquaintance, he was also a cat that walked alone, always with something withheld. I can think of no man who would have known him fully.

And so I beg you assure His Majesty that, though I shall do my best, he must treat whatever I say as at once true and false. False not because Christopher did not spy for my master, Mr Secretary, Sir Francis Walsingham, nor because he did not die by the knife near the end of May 1593 in the old Queen's reign, at the age of twenty-nine. No, the falsehood comes from that concentration on him which inevitably puts him at the centre of the story, which he never was. To ourselves, of course, we are always the heart of our own stories, but viewed from without our stories are but parts of other men's stories, themselves but the suburbs of greater stories. If we are lucky – as I was then – we may have dwelt on the fringes of epics. But as individuals we are clods of mud dropped from the wheel of Fate, which carries us we know not where and leaves us where it pleases.

That is as true of me, of course, as of him. And even of you, sir, if I may hazard, however exalted your position at Court, however much you now bask in the King's favour. Although in my world, which Christopher briefly shared, I was close to the heart of affairs, it could all have happened without me. Sir Francis would have found some other man to decipher codes and assist him as I did, and events would still have fallen out as God ordained. Not that Christopher Marlowe would have agreed with that, having little time for God's ordinances. In his world, the world of playhouses, players and poets, I had no part, of course. I thought it ungodly and unruly and, in any case, numbers, not words, were always my passion. You might discover more about him if you could find another player still living. But they never last long.

I could begin with our first meeting when he was a callow scholar of Corpus Christi, Cambridge, aged about seventeen. Except that Christopher was never callow; he was always knowing, assessing, judging, even as a youth. I remember him then as neither short nor tall, with brown hair and eyes and just the beginnings of a beard. His face was unmarked and his voice low, a Kentish drawl, unlike his writings which as perhaps you know are high-flown and exclamatory, full of energy.

But to begin at the beginning would mislead you because it would appear that my knowledge of him advanced incrementally, step by step over years, whereas that is not how we know people. We meet someone, we form an opinion and there they stay, pinned to the wall of memory unless

3

illuminated by some new event or encounter, a flash of lightning which shows them from a different angle or facing another way. We think we know what they are but we know not what they may be. It was so with me and Christopher and it is true of ourselves, of all of us.

Or I could start with his end, that flash of steel, last of several in his short life. When people still spoke of him that is what they wanted to hear about. Could that be His Majesty's interest? No, of course, you cannot say. But if I started with his end it would mislead you by giving the impression that everything before was leading up to it, a causal chain, one thing leading to another. Indeed, in those days there were some who even suspected a conspiracy. I hope I can set His Majesty's mind at rest on that. Truth and life are always more haphazard than we like to think. There was no determination in Christopher's death, no series of causes, still less any plot or design, in my opinion. Yet, looking back on it now, it seems to me it was inevitable. Inevitable but not necessary, if you accept my distinction. It was in his character to die young and in a violent manner. He need not have, he could have chosen differently, but given what he made of himself he was destined to burn bright and be abruptly extinguished. It is impossible to imagine him fading away like the rest of us, unless we imagine him as someone quite different. Similarly, you could say of me that it was inevitable I should eke out my closing years in a little room in the King's Bench prison, with its barred window and smoking candles and small coals. Inevitable that I should never burn bright, like him, but splutter long and slow, fading. But it was never necessary because I could have managed my life differently, I could have chosen differently, but that I did not, would not.

Lust in age is a little fire in a dark field, wrote another poet, one I believe Christopher knew. It is true also of life in age, but he never lived long enough to see that. He bled out on Eleanor Bull's floorboards in full combustion, the flames of life still roaring and leaping. He never knew decline, unlike me, and I cannot conceive how he would have lived with it. He would not have been Christopher if he had.

So I shall start neither at his beginning nor his end but five or six years after we first had dealings with each other, which was when I began to realise he was not the straightforward young man I had taken him for. True, we had already shared dramatic times resulting from the actions of treasonous men, a few of them good men but misguided, almost all of them foolish, but some capable schemers of murderous intent. Christopher was very young then and our dealings were friendly but businesslike, though signs of his complexity were there, had I paused to notice. But I was busy and merely relieved that he took to our trade naturally, as if already familiar with its crooked byways and hidden places.

Near the end of June 1587, after the Queen of Scots was executed, I was summoned to the house of my master, Mr Secretary Walsingham. Sir Francis was one of the two most powerful men of the kingdom, a man whom Queen Elizabeth always heeded although she never did love him as she loved her other faithful councillor, Lord Burghley. I think Mr

Secretary was too stern and too dark for her to love him, dark not only in counsel but in hair, beard, eye and doublet. He always wore black, as devout men did, and in jest she would call him her Moor while he, also in jest but without smiling, would call himself an Ethiop. He rarely laughed; his humour was in his words. Her Majesty preferred men with a lighter touch, gallant, ready men who flattered and flirted, but Mr Secretary never flattered, not even the Queen. His wit was quiet and his humour dry, both were best savoured in ret-rospect. He was never one to set the table at a roar, being a forward Salvationist, a man of the Godly party. He spoke his mind as plainly to the Queen as to the meanest beggar. She had the wisdom to value that but she did not always like it.

Mr Secretary lived with his wife and daughter on Seething Lane near the Tower in a large high house with a narrow front that concealed the extensive quarters hidden from the street. A house of many rooms, all dark-panelled and with so many unexpected doors, passages, steps and corners that I never felt I knew it all, though I visited often and even worked there on occasion. Sometimes Mr Secretary had prisoners lodged with him, special prisoners to whom he wanted to talk – or listen – at leisure. The house was so rambling that you never knew how many others were within. He could have lived grandly, building great houses like Lord Burghley and others at Court, but he was modest in all things. His house was like himself, of plain and modest demeanour, or front, with an interior of so many secret chambers that none could know them all. There was a fine garden at the back with a mulberry tree said to date from the reign of King John. Mr Secretary studied every plant with the same exactitude that he studied treacherous weeds in the realm. His other pleasures were hawking, music, painting and poetry, which he did much to cultivate and encourage but often out of sight, so that many who benefited from his patronage knew not whose teat had suckled them. It was at his instruction that the players' company, the Queen's Men, was founded.

I think Queen Elizabeth never forgave him for having contrived that which she herself had willed, albeit reluctantly. That is, the execution of her cousin, Mary, Queen of Scots. Sir Francis was deeper in that business than any other, as I know well through having been deep in it with him. Christopher was there or thereabouts, too, though not as deeply. But that was when he first showed himself willing to get his hands dirty.

Mr Secretary was working in his house the day I was summoned, as he often did when not attending the Privy Council or required at Court with Her Majesty. The streets around Seething Lane being crowded and noxious, favourable for breeding the plague, I took a boat downriver from Whitehall where I was working on some Spanish letters that had recently fallen into our hands. The code was slow to yield, like chipping away at rock, and I was reluctant to break concentration. But the summons was delivered in person by Francis Mylles, Sir Francis's private secretary and a good friend to me. I travelled alone, Francis having other business in Whitehall.

Mr Secretary's servants knew me, of course, and I was shown into the small room overlooking the street where there was a table, three chairs and a Geneva Bible. Mr Secretary owned at least one other Bible as well as many books of navigation and exploration and a large map of all the counties of England. Indeed, in his private study he had a globe showing all the countries and oceans of the world. He had a passion to know things. 'Knowledge is never too dearly bought,' he would say when Lord Burghley protested that we paid our agents too well.

After a while a girl came to fetch me. Like all Mr Secretary's personal staff, in London and at his country house in Barn Elms, she wore clean white linen and a short blue jacket. She led me to another study at the back of the house, not the large one with the globe. This one overlooked the garden, its single window darkened by the mulberry tree. It was cooler here than in the front room where you could feel the heat of horses and people in the street.

'If you please, sir, Thomas Phelippes, sir,' said the girl.

'Close the door behind you,' said Mr Secretary.

He was seated at a small desk end-on to the window and gestured me to the chair facing it. His face that day was even paler than usual, almost as white as his starched ruff. 'God's greetings, Thomas, I trust you are well?'

'I am, sir, thank the Lord. I trust you are?' He did not look it.

He shook his head. 'A martyr to the stone again. I have not been at Court or Council for a week, but by God's grace it begins to ease now.'

'I am glad to hear it.'

He nodded and looked down at two papers on his desk. We sat in silence. I assumed he had more decryption for me since that was my main task in his employ, as well as my main pleasure. Had I not been able to serve Her Majesty in this way I should have been in the cloth and wool trade and in the custom house with my father.

He looked up at me. 'I wish you to take a letter to Cambridge, an urgent letter. You will leave today. It is for the vice-chancellor, Dr Copcot, and for the master of Corpus Christi College, Dr Norgate. I would normally send it by messenger but I wish you to be there to ensure it is read and understood by both. If they doubt or question it in any way you must tell them there will be consequences.' He took the letter from a drawer in his desk. It was already sealed with the Privy Council seal. 'In order that you may discuss it with them you should know its import. It concerns Christopher Marlowe, the boy from Canterbury who helped us with the arrest of Campion and again more recently with Babington and his friends. You were in regular contact with him. When did you see him last?'

'Early this year, just before the trial of the Queen of Scots.' Mr Secretary had been witness to that and I was permitted to attend in acknowledgement of my work in bringing it about. My most recent sighting of Christopher, however, was not in connection with that business but at a playhouse here in London. I rarely visited the playhouses and we did not speak because we had agreed to pretend in public that we had no connection. He did not want his earlier association with us known in his world. That suited us too. 'A chance meeting only. We did not speak.'

'Corpus Christi is refusing to award him his Master of Arts degree on the grounds that he has not fulfilled the residency requirements. The master, Dr Norgate, fears he has secretly visited the Catholic seminary in Rheims in order to infiltrate priests back into England to murder the Queen and her ministers and restore Papacy here. Or become a secret priest himself. As you know' – Mr Secretary smiled very slightly, his lips parting just enough to show he still had teeth behind his black beard – 'young Master Marlowe never went to Rheims but was working here and in Paris on our behalf, under your tutorship. That accounts for his absences last year but not for this year. Those recent absences he has spent writing plays and negotiating their performance in London. He intends the stage to be his trade and in fact left Cambridge in March, journeying back just now to receive his degree. He is still there. The Privy Council signed this letter yesterday.'

I could not conceive how Mr Secretary knew all this but I knew better than to ask. His sources of information were many and various and he would never reveal one to another without need.

He laid his forefinger on the letter. 'Today is Friday and the degree ceremony is on Tuesday. Before then the college and university must understand that Her Majesty will be greatly displeased should one of her loyal subjects be punished for service on her behalf.' He took another paper from his desk, this time unsealed. 'You should ensure that they read the letter together and you are of course at liberty to read it yourself when they have opened it. You should not hesitate to intervene if they argue or fail to grasp it, telling them you have my full authority to do so. Dr Copcot, I gather from Lord Burghley, should prove helpful; Dr Norgate may quibble. But you shall brook no quibbles.' He handed me the second paper. 'This is a copy of the Privy Council minute summarising the letter. Take it with you and study it so that you fully understand the letter before they discuss it.'

I have that copy here, sir, among my papers. I shall read it to you.

Whereas it was reported that Christopher Marlowe was determined to have gone beyond the seas to Reames and there to remaine Their Lordships thought good to certifie that he had no such intent, but that in all his accions he had behaued him selfe oderlie and discreetlie whereby he had done her Majestie good service, and deserued to be rewarded for his faithfull dealing: Their Lordships request was that the rumour thereof should be allaied by all possible means, and that he should be furthered in the degree he was to take at the next Commencement: Because it was not her Majestie's pleasure that anie one employed as he had been in matters touching the benefit of his Countrie should be defamed by those that are ignorant of th'affaires he went about.

'You will leave today,' Mr Secretary concluded, 'and take my horse, Prince. You should be there tomorrow evening. The Privy Council will wish to hear on Monday that Marlowe is included in the degree ceremony. If not, there will be consequences. If they are at all reluctant, tell them those were my words.'

Mr Secretary's gaze was dark and steady and curiously impersonal, always the same whether he was contemplating one of his beloved hawks, addressing the Queen or interrogating a prisoner on the rack. He never sought to make windows into men's souls, as he would put it, his concern being truth, truth alone. 'Leave forthwith, take victuals from here and wear my livery. Be formal. The exercise will do Prince good.'

He looked even paler than when I arrived, the livid white of his cheeks contrasting with his square black beard. He made fists with his hands on the desk, knuckles whitening as he clenched. A single drop of sweat trickled down the side of his forrid. His gaze moved from me to the mulberry tree outside the window. 'You must forgive me, Thomas. I have been unwell this week, as I told you. Had I been at Council this matter would have been dealt with sooner. Now I feel the stone again, the cursed stone, sent by the Lord to punish us. As it does most assuredly.' He returned to me, his lips parting again in what he might have meant as a smile. He was clearly in great pain and control was costing him dearly. He nodded at the door. 'Ask Betty for victuals.'

Prince was a fine bay Arab, a beautiful horse. Whoever

gave him to Mr Secretary no doubt meant well but they did not know their man. Mr Secretary disliked riding and did so only when he had to, never for pleasure. It was strange that a man fearless in all things – because he feared God more, he would have said – should have been so fearful of horses. Probably he was nervous and his nerves made the horse nervous. Rather than ride he would go by river from his house at Barn Elms to Whitehall or Seething Lane. Prince spent too much time stabled.

I am but a moderate horseman myself and knew Prince would be frisky when let out, but the prospect of a long journey with him was still a pleasure. And so it proved. It was difficult at first in the London streets where the heedless crowds provoked Prince into some prancing and side-stepping. Once he reared and knocked over a coster-monger's barrow, causing the man to shout and swear prodigiously, but Sir Francis's blue livery protected me. Although few among the commons might have recognised it, they would have known it was someone important, someone not to be meddled with.

Once out of the city, however, Prince and I relaxed and enjoyed ourselves. The days were long and we made good time, spending the night at an inn in Ware. There I read again the summary of the sealed letter in my satchel, puzzling again how it had come to the notice of the Privy Council that Christopher's degree was to be withheld. It had always been me who dealt with him and I would have expected him to come to me. He must have had some other channel of communication. I own I felt some resentment, having thought we knew and trusted each other well enough for him to turn to me if he needed help.

No doubt Cambridge is much changed now. It had changed then, in the ten years since I left Trinity College. There was new building, old halls extended, and alleys and footpaths widened into thoroughfares. Scholars were everywhere, of course, their gowns billowing, but the streets were also thronged with labourers and traders, a veritable little London. I knew the vice-chancellor's lodge though not Dr Copcot himself. The servant who answered my knock was a woman, older than me, who mistook me for a menial despite my livery. I told her I had a letter for Dr Copcot. She asked for it, holding out her hand. I said I had to deliver it in person. That piqued her and she left me on the doorstep. I heard her call within, 'A messenger from London, sir.'

'Take his message,' came the reply.

She came back and held out her hand again. 'Give it to me and wait here for a reply.'

I own I am not a man of stature, though I have some standing in the secret world and have appeared with my master at Court. I am shorter than most men and my face is marked with the small pox. But I am no weakling, my hair and beard were fair and well-trimmed in those days, and a glance at my livery and at Prince tethered nearby should have told the woman that I was not the menial she thought. I was also, of course, a University man.

I spoke quietly, having found that quietness and control

of tone carries more authority than bluster. 'Tell Dr Copcot that the letter I bear is from the Privy Council, conveyed here with urgency by the wish of Mr Secretary Walsingham, whose man I am.'

That troubled her a little and she left without another word. There were hushed voices followed by heavy footsteps on floorboards. Dr Copcot was a stout man with a broad face which might have been forbidding but which creased and softened in welcome when he saw my blue coat and smart leather satchel. He bade me enter and took me to a parlour where I was served cake and sherry by the now obsequious woman. A groom was summoned to feed and stable Prince and a servant sent for Dr Norgate of Corpus Christi. It had been a long journey that day and I appreciated the refreshment.

Dr Norgate proved the opposite of Dr Copcot, a thin man with a long wrinkled turkey's neck. He also wore that bird's affronted expression as he shuffled across the floor, his hand shaking on his stick. I gave them the letter and they opened it together, sitting at the polished parlour table. Dr Copcot finished first and looked up. 'You are familiar—?'

I nodded.

'Well, it appears a mistake has been made, there is no question of that. Through the best of motives, I doubt not.' He glanced at Dr Norgate, who was still reading, bent so far his nose almost touched the page. 'And all shall soon be made good. The ceremony is on Tuesday and we must ensure—'

Dr Norgate looked up sharply. 'Marlowe's absences were

noted by many in the college. He has been absent even more than other scholars, who are quite bad enough. It sets a poor example if he goes unpunished. There are far too many absences of late, some for nefarious reasons as was suspected of him. If we ignore them we encourage them.'

Dr Copcot's broad face creased with concern. 'But where matters of state are concerned—'

'Others will not know that. They will know only that a prominent malefactor goes unpunished and indeed is treated with favour.'

I leaned forward and addressed Dr Norgate quietly and respectfully. 'I am sure, sir, that Mr Secretary is sympathetic to the college's concerns. But on matters touching the security of the state, of which it is his duty to inform Her Majesty, he is obliged to consider wider interests. He expects from me on my return a full account of your deliberations.' I put my finger on the list of names at the top of the page. 'Meanwhile, may I beg you, sir, to heed those who have put their names to this letter. That is a measure of its import.'

As well as Lord Burghley, the Lord Treasurer, they included the Lord Archbishop, the Lord Chancellor, the Lord Chamberlain and Mr Comptroller, Mr Secretary having been absent through his illness. Thus were the great cannon of the realm all trained at that moment upon Corpus Christi College. I suspected that Dr Norgate's initial reaction was prompted partly by pride and irritation at being summoned to treat with what he took to be an inconsiderable person. He was not so proud, however, as to be immutable to self-interest;

he understood full well what the letter entailed. He wiped a drip from the end of his nose and nodded. He could not bring himself to look at me but said, in little more than a whisper, 'There is time. It can be arranged.'

'And shall be,' added Dr Copcot, emphatically.

The master of Corpus Christi took his leave, briefly and gruffly. Dr Copcot offered me supper and a room in his lodgings for the night, which I was pleased to accept. But first, I said, I wanted to find Christopher Marlowe to give him the good news.

'Of course, of course, and I don't doubt you will be first with the news because Dr Norgate will not hurry to break it.' He smiled ingratiatingly. 'Please assure Mr Secretary and my Lord Burghley that I personally vouch that young Master Marlowe will be treated as well as his good service deserves.'

I caught up with Dr Norgate as he crept like some ailing insect past the porter's lodge at Corpus. I knew he would take little pleasure in speaking to me but I make it policy never to offend without good cause. The choppy seas of life throw us up against enough hard rocks without our running deliberately at them. When he saw me alongside him he nodded and would have continued, saying nothing, if I had not smiled and touched my cap. 'Thank you for your help in this matter, Master. I shall ensure that Mr Secretary knows of it.'

He stopped and faced me, without enthusiasm. 'I thank you, sir. Had we known that his absences were not for the reasons we suspected—'

'Your caution was correct, sir. And your understanding,

now that you know the circumstances, will be much appreciated.' Then I asked a question, partly through genuine interest and partly because if you ask someone's help and it costs them little, they are pleased with themselves and therefore think better of you. 'Pray tell me, Dr Norgate, do you know where I may find Dr Atkins of Trinity College? He taught me the mathematic and I should dearly like to thank him for the great benefit and pleasure it has given me.'

He stared. At first I thought he was adjusting to the idea that I too was a University man, but his eyes clouded with something like anxiety. 'Dead, sir.'

'Dead?' Dr Atkins had not made old bones. He would have been only five or six years older than me, still in his fourth decade.

'Dead.' Dr Norgate nodded as if listening for something far off. It was Death he listened for, of course, sensing the approach of that illustrious entity, as I do now. Death was indeed stalking him; he died later that year and was succeeded as master by Dr Copcot, who ensured that the scholars of Corpus Christi continued to be of assistance to us.

'I am sorry to hear it, sir. Pray then tell me where I may find Master Marlowe.'

I was directed to a ground-floor room across the quad. There were a few scholars about, gowned and waiting for dinner in hall which began at seven. The wealthier among them dispensed with sub-fusc and wore richer apparel of their own choosing, by favour of their fathers' deeper pockets. It had been the same in my day; rules were more flexible for the rich. Christopher, like me a scholarship boy, had begun with no such dispensation but latterly, with the money we paid him, he had shown a taste for more gorgeous apparel. The scholars were supposed to discourse among themselves only in Latin or Hebrew but as I passed among them I heard English phrases in the accents of London, Norfolk, Warwickshire and Wales.

The college was not full and Christopher was in his old room, the one he used to share with two Norfolk boys but for this visit at least he had it to himself. It was furnished as plainly as before, though now with only one narrow bed, plus table, chair and bookshelf, no rug and no curtains for the small window. On the table was a pewter pint pot, a couple of sharpened quills, an inkwell and some sheets of quarto, two of them written on. Christopher sat on the floor between the bed and window, his back against the wall, his legs drawn up so that his arms rested on his knees. He was dressed not as a scholar but as a man about the town – indeed, a gentleman about the town – in dark, expensive doublet and hose. In his right hand he held a long-bladed dagger, the sort duellists use for parrying. I always thought it an awkward weapon to wear at your belt but he almost always did, often – later, at least, in London – with his sword. He had occasion to use both, as I came to know all too well, but I think it was not only for that that he wore them. There was something of the peacock in Christopher; he liked to be smart, to be noticed, and it meant something for a cobbler's boy to achieve the gentlemanly status that permitted him to wear a sword in public. When

I arrived he was trimming his nails with the knife and had grown a thin red-brown beard and moustache.

Seated on the floor in similar pose but against the opposite wall was a fair young man wearing the usual scholar's sub-fusc. He had not even the beginnings of a beard and a sleepy left eye that was half closed in a permanent squint. But his features were fresh and clear and he smiled at my entrance. It was Christopher who had answered my knock on the door with the soft Latin *venite*, spoken wearily.

'I am sorry to surprise you, Christopher.' I nodded greeting to the young man.

'You don't surprise me.' Christopher smiled and got to his feet. His features, normally as thin and keen as his knife's blade, were transformed when he smiled, softening so that it was impossible not to see him as a small boy, mischievous and confiding. He nodded at the young man, who got to his feet and slipped past me through the open door with another smile and mumbled thanks.

I closed the door. 'Have I not surprised you? I have been seeing Dr Norgate and Dr Copcot on your behalf.'

'I assumed someone would. So it will all go through, then? I shall get my degree?'

'You shall.'

He sheathed his knife and stepped forward to embrace me. 'Thank you, Thomas. I fear I have nothing to offer you. I am dining in hall – as required – and it is too late to sign in a guest. Not that college dinner—'

'I am promised to dine with Dr Copcot.'

'Who I am sure will royally entertain any emissary of Sir Francis.'

I could not resist glancing at the papers on his table. Deciphering other people's correspondence being my business, the study of men's hands fascinates me. Christopher was a hurried scrawler, although his capitals were large with elaborate swoops and curves. An easy hand to copy. I had expected to see some scholarly work such as translations of Ovid – a passion of his since we first met – but it was pages of play-script, with many lines scored through. He was always lavish with ink.

'Another *Tamburlaine*?' His play of that name was already much spoken of in London. He must have written it since his work for us, while supposedly studying. He wrote fast, I do know that.

He shook his head. 'No, this one is about the work of the Devil.'

'A dangerous subject.'

'Less dangerous than writing about his opposite, don't you think? We know all about the Devil's works and we know what he is – one of us. Which is more than we can say of our dear Lord.' He hurried on before I could respond. 'But early days, early days. This one is yet to come. There will be other plays first.' He took his gown from the hook on the door, slipped it on over his tunic and stood before me as if to make a formal speech. 'Thomas, I am grateful that I shall get my degree, truly grateful. Please tell Sir Francis. I am grateful not only for myself but for my family and my patron, Sir Roger.

I should not want him to think I had been frivolous of my time here. Nor insensible to the generosity of the Archbishop Parker scholarship.'

Christopher's patron, the man who had spoken for him as a scholarship boy, was the judge, Sir Roger Manwood. Like Christopher, he was a man of Kent, known also to Mr Secretary, a Kentish man.

'We knew nothing of any difficulty until very recently. Otherwise it would have been resolved sooner. Or would never have arisen.'

'I knew nothing of it myself until I got here from London.'

'How did you—?'

'Poley. Robert Poley was here. He was returning to London and said he would ensure people knew. A favour he will doubtless remind me of one day. Never lets a favour go to waste, does our Robert.'

I imagine that is a name that means nothing to you, sir? It is forgotten by everyone now except a few relics of those days, like myself. Yet those were times when it seemed that nothing happened in the kingdom without Robert Poley's delicate fox prints discernible nearby, whether on palace lawns or in the filth of hovels. He made himself at home anywhere and was key to our disruption of the Babington plot. You know of that, surely – the plot to kill Queen Elizabeth and put Mary, Queen of Scots, on the throne? That young fool Babington went to the gallows for it without ever knowing whether his 'beloved Poley', as he still termed him, was his true friend and fellow-conspirator or his secret and most deadly enemy.

But that was Robert Poley for you, not quite a gentleman, not quite a Catholic, not quite a Protestant, nor ever quite a proven rogue. Mr Secretary even took him into his household at Barn Elms for a period in order to assess him thoroughly, but was still never quite sure of the man. That Poley served us well he acknowledged, but so thought those he betrayed on our behalf. 'I do not find but that Poley hath dealt honestly with me,' he declared to me once, 'yet I am loath to lay myself anyway open to him.'

Christopher's mention of him surprised me, though it should not have because I knew Poley got everywhere. 'Poley? What was Poley doing in Cambridge?' I asked.

'What Poley does everywhere, pursuing his own mysterious purposes. You must know him better than I. If I had asked he would either have invented a lie or he would have told the truth, not because it was true but because he saw advantage in my knowing. Thus he is essentially false even when true. So I didn't ask and he didn't volunteer.' He smiled and shrugged. 'Yet I cannot dislike the man. There's something about an honest knave so long as he has charm, don't you think?' He looked at me, his eyes still smiling. 'Not jealous, are you, Thomas?'

'Of course not, why should I be?' But he had hit the mark, as usual.

It was true that I neither liked nor trusted Poley but we could not ignore him. He was one of our best and most flexible agents, adept at talking his way into almost anyone's confidence. In Paris he ingeniously got himself recruited by the exile Thomas Morgan, Queen Mary's chief intelligencer, equivalent of Sir Francis on our side. Through Poley we identified many of Morgan's agents, the English Catholics lured to France to be turned into priests and secretly sent back into the kingdom to undermine us. The seedmen of sedition, Sir Francis called them. So deep was Poley in the Babington Plot – which should really be called the Ballard Plot since Ballard the priest was the prime mover – and hence so exposed to suspicion that afterwards Mr Secretary had him imprisoned for a while to conceal his role. Yet even in gaol he contrived to live comfortably and seduce a good woman who visited.

I believe he had as little natural affection for me as I for him. His charm did not work on me. We never had hard words, still less came to blows, but he was wary of me because I enjoyed Mr Secretary's confidence. He knew too that while he dealt in the secrets men told him, I knew what they told others and knew too what they secretly wrote, including what they wrote of him. His wariness probably protected me from his outright enmity.

I told Christopher of my meeting with Dr Norgate and Dr Copcot and what the Privy Council letter had said.

'That will be an arrow in Dr Norgate's eye,' he said. 'It is not just for my absences that he is against me. Others have been absent for as long but their degrees were not threatened.'

'He thought you were defecting to Rheims to become a Catholic.'

'They say that of anyone they don't like. No, the good

doctor has taken against me because he thinks I mock true Godliness and because I mix with players here in Cambridge. The authorities here think plays and players bring disrepute upon the town and would like to ban them. Also, they know that my *Tamburlaine* has great success in London and there is nothing our tutors resent more than the worldly success of their scholars. We suffer a plague of religious caterpillars here, crawling over us, hypocrites all. Was it so in your day?'

The Puritan influence in Cambridge was certainly growing. Riding in, I had observed shoals of sober, solemn, surly young men walking slowly with heads bowed, their gowns wrapped about them like so many beetles. In my day, which was only ten years before, scholars were more boisterous and often far from sober. 'Not like this. But you are not against the true religion, surely?'

He hesitated. 'How could I be?' His tone was playful and I had the impression he had considered a different reply.

'It is the Puritans you dislike?'

'Evangelists, I dislike all evangelists and all evangelising.'

'Even those who evangelise what you yourself believe?'

'I've never met anyone who believes what I believe.'

I did not then ask what that was. In those years Puritans and other dissenters were vigorously pursued by Archbishop Whitgift. He hanged a couple of Christopher's Cambridge contemporaries because they would not accept the settlement under Queen Elizabeth. Mr Secretary also vigorously pursued dissenters and extremists, despite himself being an evangelist of the Protestant cause. His target was anyone who threatened the security of the state, Protestant or Catholic or free-thinker. If he asked me what Christopher believed, as he had of others whose loyalty he probed, I should have been compelled to tell him that I did not know but that Christopher sometimes appeared to reject all religion. Better therefore that I really did not know, so I didn't push Christopher to explain. But I wanted to know. This wasn't the first time we had had this kind of conversation but I had never known him so explicit. I fingered the papers on his table. 'So this is your Devil play?'

'Notes and sketches, small beer. A German scholar sells his soul to the Devil for worldly riches and triumphs. Hell awaits but he cannot bring himself to repent. Not a new story but mine will be like no other.'

'Prodigal of ink and paper.'

'They'll pay for themselves.'

'Not heretical, is it? If you write of heresies you'll be accused of believing them.'

'In which case I shall simply ensure that the heretics in my plays are woefully punished.'

'I hear your *Tamburlaine* is a fine and bloody play. Much spoken of in London.'

He told me he had a new manner of writing verse for players and enthused about the ancients, particularly Ovid. He always came back to Ovid or Lucan, mainly Ovid. I encouraged such talk because it brought out another side of him, a side I liked, a fine disinterested passion. Christopher's usual manner was quiet, often distant, sometimes mocking and disdainful, or coldly scornful when provoked. But when it came to Ovid and the ancients his speech gained in pace and warmth as if they were close friends. I think they were; for him, all literature was contemporary. He delighted in anyone who showed interest, his brown eyes moistening and brightening. Showing interest was all I could do, sadly, having forgotten most of what I learned of the ancients in favour of my own passion for numbers and symbols. But he would ask about that and I would try to convey the purity of their appeal, their cleanliness, logic and mystery, uncontaminated by the detritus of humanity. I confessed I could never read slowly enough to relish poetry.

It was no bar between us. He could imagine, he said, the beauty of number, the delight of an elegant solution. He speculated that his new way of writing verse with few rhymes resembled the mathematic in that he made patterns from the music and rhythm of words. We were talking thus when the bell rang for dinner. He pulled his gown about him. 'Thank you again for your help. Please pass on my gratitude and respect to Sir Francis.'

'Shall you return to London after the ceremony on Tuesday? We might have more work for you if you are not too taken up with your plays.' I had in mind fresh evidence of Spanish invasion plans I had recently decrypted. Already busy, we were about to become much busier.

He took my hand. 'Thomas, you are an unlikely agent of the Devil. All the more effective for it.'

'You think our work is the work of the Devil?'

'Possibly, but without your knowing it.'

'You are a Papist after all, then?' I did not mean that seriously.

'Worse, worse than that. Worse than you think.' He laughed. 'Don't worry, I heard enough from Huguenots who fled to Canterbury to render me proof against Papism. If Her Majesty calls me to arms again, of course I should respond. You will find me in Shoreditch. Just ask among the players.'

When later Christopher was accused of free-thinking I recalled these remarks without realising I had remembered them. Around the time of his death, lines from his plays were quoted as evidence of atheistical free-thinking and Machiavellism but while he was still in Cambridge most of those lines had not then been written. However, public display of such sentiments was dangerous and I cautioned him against it, though I now think the danger was partly what attracted him. What I did not know then was the effect he would have on my own beliefs.

Could this be the reason for the King's interest in him, sir? Of course, you cannot say, I accept that. But it would be an understandable interest. I hear His Majesty's proper fear and love of God does not preclude him from exploring the minds of men?

Anyway, there was a more immediate sequel to that conversation. It occurred after chapel the following morning. I attended the Corpus Christi service rather than my own old college's or the Vice Chancellor's, partly to impress on Dr

Norgate that the eye of the state was upon him and partly because I wanted to see more of Christopher. I confess to you now that I felt a fondness for Christopher, I always had. I felt drawn to him as if he needed protecting, a notion he would have scorned, of course. Not in the sense in which protection is normally understood – he was well capable of looking after himself in this world – but I felt he needed protection from himself. For all his knowingness and cleverness, for all his readiness to attack or defend with wit or blade or fists, there was something vulnerable about him. I cannot even now say precisely what it was but it had to do with honesty, honesty regardless of consequence, and a curious gap in his self-awareness. God spare us for it, sir, but I think you will agree that most of us are frequently dishonest in small things, sometimes in big things? But not Christopher. He would deceive only with deliberation, only to higher purpose such as the security of the state in the work he did for us, never to his own advantage. In himself, in his beliefs and natural reactions, he was as spontaneous and unguarded as a child. Perhaps that was why he seemed vulnerable, as if he needed saving from himself. As indeed his end proved. But why I felt I had to protect him, I cannot say. In view of that end, you might say I failed.

And so I worshipped that morning in Corpus Christi with all the scholars. The singing was lusty and Dr Norgate preached a good sermon on obedience to God and the Queen, to our parents, to the teaching of the Bible and to conscience. He argued that submission is key, submission to God's will, and that only in renouncing ourselves do we truly find ourselves. He could not have intended this for my benefit since he did not know I would be there, but I thought it merited favourable report to Sir Francis. Would such a sermon find favour now, sir? You think so? I hope you are right. I hear that Dr Donne, Dean of St Paul's, preaches a goodly sermon, though I believe he has also penned some scandalous verses. He was a Catholic, you know, before repenting. I regret that my circumstances prevent me from hearing him though I fear my soul may be past benefitting now.

It was another fine morning and after the service people stood talking in the quad. I had spotted Christopher near the front of the chapel but lost him as we came out, then saw him again walking rapidly out of the college, alone. I caught up with him on the street, which was filling with dispersing congregations. He acknowledged me curtly, without slackening his pace.

'A good sermon,' I said.

'Keeps the sheep happy.' He walked on, looking straight ahead.

'But it's true, is it not? That only by renouncing ourselves do we find our true selves?'

'The truth of it doesn't matter. So long as it stops you thinking for yourself its purpose is achieved.'

I stopped in the street. 'You really think that is its purpose?'

He turned to me with a sigh, forcing others to step around us. 'I am sorry, Thomas, I am not in a giving mood this morning. I've no time for these hypocrites. Follow me to the river if you wish. Walking by water is balm for the soul.' He turned again and walked on.

I was surprised and affronted. It was ungracious, given what I had just done for him, and there had been nothing in the sermon to which any good Christian could take exception. But I decided he should be taken to task and hurried after him into one of those alleys leading to the river. It was busy with worshippers, mostly gowned scholars spilling like plagues of beetles from court and quad, and was too narrow to walk two abreast, so I was forced to follow until it broadened out and we could talk again. He did not acknowledge me at first but strode on, looking neither right nor left, his face set hard. It was as if he had received an insult and was on his way to give someone a beating.

'Forgive me, Thomas,' he declared suddenly, still without looking at me. 'It is the Devil in me. That is all. It will pass. He will leave while we walk.'

'The Devil possesses you? Does he visit often?'

'Only in worship. Divine service prompts rebellion in my breast. It has since childhood. I kneel, I sing, I pray with the rest but my heart rebels within me. It is not the message but being preached at. And being expected to believe the impossible.'

'What is impossible? You are not suggesting that Our Lord—'

'I am suggesting that every day since God created the world the sun has risen in the morning and set in the evening. But we are asked to believe that one day it set at the sixth hour

31

and rose again at the ninth hour, a unique event in nature coinciding with the crucifixion of Our Lord. Do you believe that, Thomas? Do you? Tell me honestly.'

He turned to face me now, his dark eyes challenging. For a few moments I was lost for an answer, which prompted him to launch a sermon of his own. He queried the age of the world as estimated by the Fathers of the Church, then said that holy scripture suggested that Jesus had a mistress, then that He had an unnatural relationship with the disciple John and finally that if we gave all our goods to the poor as the scriptures urge us then the poor would become the rich and we the poor. They would then be urged to give back to us what we had given to them and we would go on changing places for ever. 'So the Kingdom of Heaven on earth is nothing more than a perpetual dance, a merry-go-round,' he concluded.

We were by then at the riverside. The more eagerly Christopher spoke, the slower he walked. Expounding heresies excited him. But it also lightened his mood and by the end he was smiling at his own exuberance. I was in something of a daze, not only because such heresies were shocking but because they were disturbing. I had never suspected him of harbouring such thoughts. I perceive they still have power to shock, sir? Dare you relay them to the King? Is it this that His Majesty wishes to know about?

Christopher's own deepest beliefs? I fear I cannot plumb him deep enough to know what he truly believed. If anything. He loved playing with ideas, you see, especially ideas with power to shock, and it was hard to know how he stood behind them, whether far or near. As I said when we began today, he was a cat that walked alone.

At the time I comforted myself by reflecting that he was at least partly in jest, a comfort reinforced when he placed his hand on my shoulder again and smiled his soft smile, 'Forgive me, Thomas, I did not mean to burden you with troublesome fantasies. There is enough to complicate life without idle speculations. It is time we broke our fast.'

CHAPTER TWO

Cambridge? Did Cambridge change him? A shrewd question, sir, one I cannot comfortably answer. He once told me that study of the ancients taught him to question everything. But of course he had studied them at school in Canterbury so where the change began I cannot say. It may have been Cambridge, though he did not speak in this manner when I first met him some six years before the events I have just related. He was new to Cambridge when we met.

In those days I did my secret work for Sir Francis in a private study in Whitehall Palace called the New Library, although it held more maps than books. Sir Francis and Lord Burghley were keen geographers and spent much time studying maps, Lord Burghley especially when he feared the Queen apt to be persuaded by some handsome sea-captain to pay for voyages in distant seas. He was parsimonious with the Queen's money, as I now know to my cost, and his broad, hunched figure would stand as if turned to salt before a map. Sometimes he wrote on the maps or altered them according to what returning sea-captains – those who did return – reported. Sir Francis too would study them for hours on end until he knew all foreign countries and regions. But his chief study was a map of English counties on which were marked the houses of recusant Catholic families suspected of harbouring priests and other seditious men. This was the map he later removed to his house in Seething Lane, along with the large globe.

None apart from those two men and the Earl of Leicester, and those working closely with them, were allowed in the New Library. The Earl of Essex gained entry as a result of the Queen's favour but he did not come often. As one of the few granted regular access I worked on my decipherings at a small table in the corner, locking my papers away when not engaged on them so that as few as possible should know whose letters we read.

That little room gave me the privacy and quiet I needed. And my need was great during the busy early summer of 1581. I was recently returned from Paris, whither Sir Francis had sent me to help our ambassador there, Sir Henry Cobham, with some papers that had come into his hands. They were not, it turned out, so very important, being copies of Spanish correspondence about the fate of 500 Spanish soldiers who had landed in County Kerry the year before in order to raise an Irish insurrection. They had surrendered in September and our forces had massacred all but 23 of them. It was not clear how or why they were massacred but what was clear from these papers was that the Spanish Court still did not know the fate of their expedition. That was important because it meant we could reasonably assume there was no Spanish spy in our midst.

Sir Francis was also recently returned from Paris where he had been sent by the Queen on a mission of great delicacy – negotiating Her Majesty's possible marriage to the Duc d'Anjou. I daresay, sir, that few even now know that such a possibility was ever on the table? Or under it. Mr Secretary's task was made even more delicate by the fact that he found it impossible to establish whether Her Majesty was serious. A further complication was that he himself was deeply opposed to it, believing that the throne of England should not be shared with any foreigner, especially a Catholic foreigner. But there was a point beyond which no one, not even Sir Francis, durst argue with Her Majesty. She knew his opinion and he privately hoped that she chose him as her negotiator because she wanted to show willing but did not really want the negotiation to succeed. Sir Francis appointed his young cousin, Thomas Walsingham – who later became Christopher's patron, as you shall hear – to be his confidential courier. I was involved because correspondence carried by Thomas had to be encoded. Also, I knew more than I was supposed to because my intimate role in Sir Francis's affairs meant that other men assumed I knew everything – which I did not – and so would discuss matters freely with or before me.

As well as all this we were dealing with serious threats on our own soil. The Pope had recently issued dispensation to Catholics to swear false loyalty to the Queen without endangering their souls. His predecessors, of course, had already granted dispensation to murder her and her advisers in order to restore England to the old faith.

Do you know whether these dispensations still stand, sir, or did lapse with the death of the Queen? No? It should be known. If anyone doubts their seriousness, remember the plot to destroy the government and parliament with gunpowder in 1605. I am sure King James will remember that business, a very close thing. I was myself called back to help with it, then abandoned again afterwards.

To return to my story: we had learned of new plots against the life of the Queen. Some were serious, others the fantasies of strange or lonely minds, others again the vengeful desires of men consumed by grievance. As always, the mad were made use of by the bad and part of my duty was to weigh the seriousness of these threats, sifting evidence in the New Library.

Even that, however, was not my main concern that summer. This was a secret Jesuit mission into our realm to recruit young men to be trained abroad as priests who would then return to fan the embers of discontent. We knew the mission was launched, we knew the English priests who led it – Robert Persons and Edmund Campion – and that at least one other priest was infiltrated with them. We knew too that they had recruited seven young men to send secretly to the seminary at Rheims. All this was from correspondence one of our spies had been entrusted with, which I had copied and deciphered. But we had no idea where in the kingdom these men were nor the names they used, though we did know that Campion passed himself off as a jeweller and Persons as a military man.

I was working on this one summer morning when Nicholas Faunt burst into the New Library. I say 'burst' because Nicholas, a busy, bustling hirsute man who was one of Sir Francis's private secretaries, never merely entered a room but immediately seemed to fill it. 'Thomas, you are bidden with me to Barn Elms,' he said loudly. 'Mr Secretary has a task for you. It is urgent, we must leave now.'

He had a boat waiting. The tide was against us and so the journey took longer than it should have, which gave more time for Nicholas to tell me what was afoot. He was not supposed to, of course, but he was one of those self-important men keen for you to know that he knew things you didn't. He couldn't resist hinting at them and, provided you didn't show too much curiosity, might eventually tell you half the story unprompted. It was a serious failing in a private secretary but he was loyal, energetic and efficient, and otherwise served his master well. Thus I learned that my task involved the insertion of a spy into a group of conspirators. It had to be someone entirely unsuspected, an apparent sympathiser uncontaminated by previous involvement with us. Nicholas had himself suggested this particular spy, a man a few years younger than himself whom he had known at school in Canterbury and who was now at Corpus Christi College, Cambridge, where Nicholas himself had been. His name was Christopher Marlowe. He was apparently well versed in theology, familiar enough with the ways of the old faith to pass for a Catholic while remaining soundly Protestant. But he was not extremely so, he was no Puritan.

'He is a scholarship boy, he needs money, as does his family, he is willing and discreet,' said Nicholas. 'Term has ended and the college supposes him travelling home to Canterbury, as he will after the excursion we intend for him. Mr Secretary has interviewed him and pronounced him suitable.'

'Where is the excursion?'

'That I am not at liberty to say.' Nicholas compressed his lips and gazed across the rippling grey water. He was trying to imply that telling me would be a step too far but I suspected he didn't know and didn't like to admit it. So it proved when Sir Francis received me alone in the study of his great house at Barn Elms, overlooking the orchards towards the river. 'Nicholas has doubtless revealed to you what you are to do.'

'Only in part, sir.'

There was almost a smile. 'What he won't have told you is that you are to take the young man into Berkshire, to a house sometimes called Moore Place, otherwise Lyford Grange, near Wantage, about half a day's ride from Oxford. The owner is Francis Yate, a gentleman who is currently visiting the Tower as a guest of Her Majesty. His house has long been a hive of recusants. They hide priests and hold masses there and also house some English nuns who earlier fled to Belgium, but have now returned because of the persecutions. Our quarries, the two Jesuits Persons and Campion, are somewhere in that area and I suspect may seek temporary refuge in Lyford Grange. Not a wise choice since it is widely known for what it is, but they are not well-versed in secret ways and Campion particularly is of an open and free nature. Secrecy is not natural to him. A man called George Eliot is charged by the sheriff with security in the area and will be investigating the household. He will not know that you are in the area and you should have nothing to do with him. Apart from our young man, there will be another agent, a man called Frizer, deployed by my Lord Leicester to gain access to the house. He is Leicester's man, nothing to do with us and you must have nothing to do with him either. Your task is to insert Master Marlowe into that household without anyone suspecting him. We need our own man there. Or woman.'

The search for these two Jesuits had been my main concern for some weeks. They had landed at Rye in Sussex and then disappeared. How Mr Secretary should have known they were in Berkshire I had no idea, but like the fox he knew many things and no one but him was privy to all.

'They were recently in Oxford or thereabouts,' he continued. 'Campion has written a paper, his "Ten Reasons" paper, arguing for Catholicism against Protestantism and asserting that Her Majesty has no right to occupy the throne of England. It was probably printed at Stonor, a Catholic house near Henley. Two days ago four hundred copies were left on the pews of St Mary's church in Oxford for scholars to find when they arrived to defend their theses. It had considerable effect since there are many Catholics in Oxford, open and secret, as you know. Indeed, Campion himself was a fine Oxford scholar and like to become a great figure in our English Church until he defected to Rome.' Mr Secretary looked down, nodding to himself. 'It is a good paper, well-argued and powerfully seditious, as you would expect. Take it and read it.' He handed me a copy across his desk, smiling slightly at my surprise and discomfiture. 'You worry that it is a treasonous offence to possess such a paper, but don't, it is permitted us. We must study our enemies, Thomas. We must know their arguments in order to fortify our own. And Father Edmund Campion is a man deserving of respect, a Godly and able man gone wrong, which is why he must be destroyed. And you must destroy this copy when you have read it. It would not do to have it bruited abroad.'

I was to find Marlowe at an inn in Wantage and agree with him a plan of action. Before I left Mr Secretary warned me against the other agent sent to the house. 'Ingram Frizer will be anxious to prove himself useful to the Earl of Leicester. As will George Eliot, the sheriff's man, who will want to advance his career. The household will hate and fear them. They are rough men, unlike your scholar. Because he is gentle in manner he will have a better chance of gaining the confidence of the household, which is why it is best Eliot and Frizer know nothing of him. Nor he of them. The Earl of Leicester will anyway inform us of anything they report.'

It was true that Christopher was quiet and usually gentle in manner but, as I was to find, he had harder rock within than Leicester's bullies.

I was given a horse from the Barn Elms stable – not Prince, unfortunately – and left to find my own way early the following morning. This may not seem a great matter to anyone familiar with the highways and byways to the west of London but I knew the roads to Paris better than our own and my short-sightedness means I must depend upon the directions of others, who are not always accurate or honest. Thus it took me the better part of two days to find Wantage, after spending an uncomfortable night in a hovel near Henley, persecuted by fleas. Their bites still marked me when I reached the inn, which at least looked a more respectable place. There was a boy sitting on the bench outside, reading. He stood at my approach and I asked for Master Marlowe who was lodging there.

'I will send for him, sir. Meanwhile, may I show you to your room?'

It was gratifying to find I was expected. Mr Secretary thought of everything. I gave my horse to the ostler and followed the boy up the dark twisting stairs to a light pleasant room overlooking the road. It had a bed and an undulating floor of broad polished oak planks. The boy pointed. 'Mr Marlowe is to share the bed with you, sir.'

'Where is he?'

'He is here, sir.'

It took me a second to realise as he smiled at my puzzlement. He had no trace of a beard in those days and his face was even more boyish. He wore the plain black of a scholar, which in my tired unthinking state I had taken for a servant's livery. His hair was dark and long.

'I thought you would prefer we talk here in private,' he said.

'You thought well, Master Marlowe.' We shook hands.

Conversation that evening was fuelled by wine and leg of lamb. I had been given money for expenses and, having seen the colour of my coin, our host was assiduous. When I asked Christopher what he knew of our task, he said, 'To catch secret priests. That is all I have been told.'

'And you are happy to do that?'

'As happy to do that as anything.'

I interpreted that as meaning anything for money. I was wrong. Of course, as a poor scholar money mattered to him and it was to prove a powerful determinant in his life, significant in his death. But it was never his prime motive for working for us, as it was for many. Precisely what his motives were, I cannot say. He had no love for Popery and I am sure that he loved his country, though he would never have put it in those terms. He loved excitement, too, and was not averse to experimenting with himself.

Anyway, I was not exploring the recesses of Christopher's personality that first evening. I explained that his task was to penetrate Lyford Grange, reporting to me on who was there and on anything he learned. In particular, he was to listen for any hint that the two priests, Persons and Campion, were in the area. We discussed how he might present himself at the house and I was outlining various ruses when he cut me off with an assurance that might have been offensive in one so young, but for his enthusiasm.

'Surely I must be a secret Catholic in search of others,'

he said. 'And, since the truth is the best concealment, I should stick as close to it as possible. I should be a scholar at Cambridge unhappy with its Reformist sympathies, travelling to Oxford in hope of privately hearing more Catholic teaching. Some of my fellows, secret Catholics, have gone abroad to seminaries where they will become priests before returning to spread the word here, but I have not the means to travel and am less bold than they. Thus, my hosts may see me as someone who may be worked upon to aid the cause.'

'And how have you found your way to Lyford Grange? Why here?'

'I travelled from Cambridge to London with some fellows. I left them in London to come secretly to Oxford, following the river and hoping to call at Stonor House near Henley, having heard it is a stout Catholic stronghold. But I heard too that it is surrounded by spies and informers so I determined to continue to Oxford. I am greatly wearied and, having learned there were pious nuns at Lyford Grange, hoped I might rest for a while here. I can pay for my sustenance.'

'And who are you? If you are Christopher Marlowe of Canterbury and Corpus Christi and you come under suspicion you will be a marked man for life.'

'I am Robin Noakes of Rye in Sussex. He was a fellow scholar who died a week before the end of term. They will not distinguish my Kentish from a Sussex accent. You have to have been born in either to know the difference.'

'You have been busy thinking.'

'It is what I do.'

He proved a natural. Most needed schooling in how to seek truth through falsehood but Christopher sprang from his chrysalis fully formed. He was never at a loss to explain himself. He could give twenty different explanations for what he was doing or where or why, often more convincing than the truth. Sometimes he would do it in jest, challenging you to guess the correct explanation and laughing at your failures.

He was also armed with a knife, I noticed. That was not in itself unusual, of course – we all carried knives for cutting our bread and meat and to protect ourselves if necessary – but the blade in Christopher's belt was a dagger, the long, pointed kind held in a dueller's left hand to parry while he attacked with his rapier in his right hand. I pointed at it. 'Devout scholars do not carry daggers like that.'

He glanced at it almost affectionately as if it were a puppy or kitten. 'I'll leave it behind. I have a smaller one. I usually wear this when travelling. In case of need.'

It was true that one had to take care when travelling, then as now, whether journeying far or walking the streets of London, but I do believe I never saw Christopher without knife or – later – sword. Except when he was killed. Even then he used a knife, though not his own.

We set off for Lyford Grange early the following morning. It was east of Wantage and not a long walk. There was no need for me to accompany him, of course – indeed, he should not be seen with me by anyone there – but I wanted to view the place discreetly and to find some secluded spot where messages could be left or where we could meet. That was not easy because the house, a fine modern moated building, was set amid the flat lands of those parts and not overlooked from high ground. I durst not go closer than where I could see the roofs and chimneys through the trees. There was a copse just off the path, mainly ash and elm, in the middle of which we found a solitary old oak in its own small clearing. It had a dry bole near the ground about the size and depth of a man's hand. We agreed to leave messages there, covering them with bark. I would check it at six o'clock that evening, again at eight the following morning and again at six the following evening. Christopher would meet me there if he could get away and needed to speak. When he finally left the house he would pretend to head for Oxford, about thirteen miles away, but would circle back to me at the inn. I tried to get him to go through his cover story again but he cut me short.

'Don't worry, I know what I'm doing.'

Even as a youth he was never less than sure of himself. Perhaps too sure. I didn't want to unsettle him when he was about to strut his piece on stage, as it were, so I merely nodded and bade him have a care.

He walked through the trees back to the path, his leather pouch slung across his shoulder. He did not look back. He never did.

There being no message that evening, I assumed he had gained entry and been allowed to stay. There was nothing for me to do but to enjoy a ramble through the fields and a good dinner of mutton washed down with ale. Waiting forms a large part of our work, along with patience and attention to detail, and I have known more promising cases ruined by haste and impetuosity than by any other cause. I have never minded waiting, especially in the comfort of a good inn. Having no deciphering to occupy me, I devised that evening a scheme to enhance my father's and my own riches through our work at the custom house, where my father was collector of petty customs as well as of tonnage and poundage on exports. I thought it a fair and just scheme and it was indeed to prove lucrative, though it led ultimately to my spending years in cells such as this.

CHAPTER THREE

Nor was there a message the following morning. I spent the day pottering, planning my new customs scheme and gossiping with mine host's wife who bemoaned how the larger houses of the area, including the Grange, were very busy with many comings and goings and much hospitality, yet brought no business to the inn. 'The fine ladies and gentlemen who stay there have no truck with us,' she lamented. 'Not even their servants, they keep theirselves to theirselves as if the rest of us had the plague.'

I thought again it was time I found a wife of my own, some kind soul to keep house for me and comfort me at night. Someone to rear children who would look after us in our old age, as I was already beginning to do with my own father.

'And what be your business here, sir?' she asked. 'And your young friend who was here before you? Will he be coming back?'

'My nephew,' I said. 'He has gone to the university to find a college that will admit him next year. When he returns we will continue our journey to London where we are employed in the custom house.'

Lying is both a natural and acquired facility which comes easier to some than to others. You must have observed this at Court, sir? It was never difficult for me. In those days I always had a cover story at hand to explain myself, except when I could proudly assert that I was on Mr Secretary Walsingham's business. It came easily then but as I grew older I wearied of it and now I find pretence no longer a pleasure or excitement but a burden, another thing to have to remember. That is why I am unafraid to tell you truth now, sir, no matter what the consequences. But it would help to know the reason for your interest?

No matter. I went to the oak tree that evening and scrabbled around in the bole but again found no note. I was fearing that something might have gone wrong when a voice said, 'Seek and ye shall find.'

Christopher was sitting above me on a bough shaped as if God had designed it for the reclining human form. He climbed down, dusting off his black breeches. 'Don't worry, I haven't slept here all night. But it would be more comfortable than the truckle bed I have in that house.'

'They accepted you?'

'They love me.'

They had admitted him reluctantly at first, questioning his background. He had convinced them that he smouldered – that was the word he used – beneath the damp Protestant cloud over Cambridge, which blocked off all light from the old faith. He had heard that Oxford was more enlightened, that there were sympathetic scholars there prepared to preach in private the truths publicly disavowed by today's dour evangelism. He wanted to hear them. He was helped by the fact that a shoal of Oxford scholars had arrived that morning to see the nuns and to partake of the Mass with Father Campion, they said. Thus he learned that Campion had indeed been there, that he had left at dawn the day Christopher arrived, that the eight nuns present – he had their names by heart – had been so mesmerised by his preaching that they had remained on their knees long after he had urged them to rise.

'So the bird has flown. Do they know where?'

'They know that Father Persons had instructed him to ride to Lancashire to retrieve certain documents and then to hide with sympathisers in Norfolk. But they think he will return sooner. They have sent a rider to beg him back for one more night to preach to the multitude now gathered and longing to hear him. He is forbidden by Persons to stay longer but, it being Sunday tomorrow, they hope he will say Mass and preach a sermon before departing again. There are about sixty there, with hardly a floorboard in the house to sleep on. Some will have to sleep in the garden.'

Apart from the nuns, the household comprised two chaplains, Mrs Yate and her staff and a number of other visitors. The influx of local Catholics and scholars had fortunately swamped Christopher's arrival and he had found himself ignored after initial questioning. He was now simply one of many and could come and go as he pleased. He had taken the precaution of ostentatiously quizzing the scholars about Oxford.

'Have you any other names?' I was thinking of Frizer, the Earl of Leicester's man.

'None. There are many whose names I do not know and I cannot afford to appear curious. They mention one George Eliot, some sort of sheriff's man or enforcer who sniffs around, but I haven't met him.'

'You must try to stay until Campion returns, if he does.'

'What do you want me to say to him?'

'You don't need to say anything. Just let me know he's there. Then we can arrest him. Or this George Eliot can.'

'Arrest?'

'Of course. What else should we do?'

He nodded. 'Of course, that is what it must come down to. I've always thought Judas deserved more credit than we give him. Why he did it, I mean.'

'Thirty pieces of silver, was it not?' Some spy for money openly and shamelessly, others do the same but pretend other reasons. Christopher was being paid but I didn't know how much and assumed this to be a preliminary to a request for more.

'I'm not sure thirty pieces was sufficient motivation in his case.'

'You think he should have held out for more?'

'No. I think he had another reason.'

'Loyalty to the scribes and Pharisees, to Judaism?'

'More complicated than that.'

That was all we had time for. The following day being the Sabbath, I anticipated no message and no Christopher, there being little opportunity to escape from such a religious household on a Sunday morning. But I still went to the tree. It was another fine morning and dappled sunlight filtered through the branches. After checking the bole I lingered, observing the wood anemones and other examples of God's handiwork. It was too late for bluebells, my favourite, but I suspected there must have been plenty. Then I climbed the tree to the bough from which Christopher had surprised me, intending to rest a while. It was even more comfortable than it looked and I nodded off.

I awoke to hear hooves and men's voices on the path. I couldn't see them nor could I hear what they said as they spoke low. I climbed down and crept through the under-growth until I could see the flank of a horse through the branches, with a man's leg in the stirrup. Beside it were the head and shoulders of another man talking up to the rider, whose upper body I could not see. The man on the ground had one hand on the horse's mane and was gesticulating with the other. He had an unkempt red beard, untidy brown hair and some kind of rusty birthmark or scar across the top of his cheek and the side of his nose. His voice was low and urgent.

'Abingdon, go to Abingdon,' he was saying. 'Find George Eliot and tell him to bring the magistrate and a force of men, as many as he can, and come with all speed. There are rich pickings here and I don't doubt he will be well rewarded.'

The other man said something I couldn't catch and Red Beard shook his head. 'Now, with all speed. Go now.' He stepped back and slapped the horse's neck as the rider turned away.

I could hear him trotting briskly along the path towards Wantage. Red Beard stood watching for a moment before turning back towards the manor. I waited for his footsteps to fade before creeping farther forward. Through the massed leaves of a holly I saw the back of him as he disappeared around a bend, a broad back, burly, clad in a brown leather tunic and clumping along in heavy riding boots. I could have followed but did not want to risk his turning and seeing me. Instead I returned to the inn.

I visited the tree again early that evening but there was still no Christopher and no message. Worried that something might have gone wrong in the manor, that he might have been discovered, I advanced through the trees towards the house, keeping parallel with the path. It was difficult to move silently through the undergrowth but I took my time and eventually had a view of it. The drawbridge was still down but there was a man watching it from one of the turrets. He took no care to conceal himself, looking outwards all the time, either down at the grounds or scanning the horizon and shielding his eyes with his hands. Twice he looked directly at the trees concealing me. I kept still. Then, while I watched and wondered what I could do – which was nothing, of course – Red Beard appeared on the far side of the draw-bridge leading a sturdy bay horse. Once across the bridge he mounted and trotted back along the path towards Wantage, passing close enough for me to smell the horse. The man in the tower watched him for a while before turning away and disappearing. He was back two or three minutes later, having presumably reported.

A few minutes later Christopher strolled out of the house onto the drawbridge. He gave the appearance of one at ease and taking the air. He crossed the drawbridge and loitered on the bank, examining the water-lilies. Then he strolled towards the trees on the other side of the path from me, fingering and examining the lower branches. Next he bent a hazel branch until it half snapped, then from beneath his tunic took out the dagger I thought he had promised to leave behind and cut the branch free. Next he strolled along the path past where I was hiding, using his knife to shape one end of the branch into a rough handle. He looked like a well-fed idler on a fine day, a youth without thought or care.

I let him pass before creeping back through the woods to our oak. He had beaten me to it but was no longer the dreamer with time on his hands. He cut off my account of how I had followed him, stabbing the ground with his stick.

'You must act now. Father Campion is here for the taking. He arrived last night and preached this morning. He said Mass, I was there. They will hide him until tomorrow. But they are watchful, suspicious of another man there, a man called Frizer. He's a bit of a ruffian but friendly with the cook with whom he used to work at the house of Thomas Roper in Canterbury, which is where I come from. Roper is grandson to Sir Thomas More, good Catholic family, which was why the cook vouched for Frizer. But they don't trust him, they suspect he might be doing what I'm doing, especially as he left suddenly on horseback just now without word to anyone.'

'Any sign that you are suspected?'

'I don't think so. He and I quarrelled.'

'How? What about? Describe him.'

He described Red Beard and I told him what I had overheard. Also, that I had been warned of him and that he worked for the Earl of Leicester. 'I didn't tell you because I didn't want to complicate your task. What was your quarrel?'

'He challenged me in front of others, asking did he not know me by sight, was I not the cobbler's son from Canterbury? I don't remember him and had no reason to think he'd recognise me but he evidently does. In which case I can't think why he'd say so publicly unless to deflect attention from himself. I denied it, of course, but he kept on about it and so I said he must know me from Cambridge where I now suddenly remembered seeing him with soldiers and burghers of the town. He'd helped arrest some scholars suspected of being Catholics about to flee abroad. He denied that of course and cuffed my head, cursing me for a lying whelp. Which was true, of course. Then we fought.'

'You fought?' The Frizer I had glimpsed was a burly grown man but Christopher looked unharmed, his skin unblemished, his skull unbroken.

'Only briefly. Others intervened. But not before I split his lip with a pewter mug.' He smiled. 'I did not pull my knife. You should be proud of me.'

That was the first sign I had that Christopher, for all his gentle airs and graceful speech, relished a fight. He used to excuse it by saying he had inherited his father's temper. Maybe he had, but I think he also enjoyed it. He had the self-control to contain himself when he wished.

We were interrupted by the sounds of horses, harnesses and marching feet from the direction of Wantage. Christopher sprang up into the oak like a monkey, standing on the bough he and I had rested upon. 'A lot of them, soldiers and burghers.' He jumped down. 'I must get back to the house.'

'No. Stay here. If they see you they'll take you for a sympathiser and arrest you.'

'That's what you want, surely? What we want, I mean. Proof I'm a loyal Papist so that Robin Noakes can ride again on Mr Secretary's behalf, unlike that Frizer whom they will now know has betrayed them.'

I hadn't realised that he saw himself as continuing in our service and wasn't at all sure that Mr Secretary envisaged that. 'You may be imprisoned or worse, especially if they find Campion there.'

'Sir Francis will see me right, won't he? You trust him, don't you?'

I had never come across such youthful enthusiasm in an agent. 'You've no idea what prison is like. You're better off here, let the searchers do their work. You've done your job.'

'I want to see it through.' He ran off through the trees.

I assume, sir, that you do not need me to describe all the events of that night? They were much trumpeted at the time and are one of the events of the old Queen's reign, along with the Armada and the more noble executions, that are spoken of still. I did not witness them myself, anyway, so could only summarise what I had from Christopher later.

Very well, sir, very well. It will add little to His Majesty's knowledge of Christopher but if it is to the King's purpose, so be it. But if I may say so, sir – if I may – a little more ale and sustenance would help. I grow weary in this close confinement, as perhaps you can see. Thank you, sir, thank you kindly.

Well, I hid in the tree until the soldiers had passed. I was tempted to creep through the trees again to spy on the house but I feared capture, having seen enough of soldiers when working in the Low Countries for Mr Secretary to know that explanations, subtleties, distinctions and fine judgements are of no account once swords are drawn. So I retreated to the inn.

Christopher did not appear until the following morning, exhausted and exhilarated and not smelling sweetly. 'I feared you had been taken,' I told him.

'I feared for myself at times, but it helps to be of little consequence.'

He told me that the soldiers mounted guard around the house and the other armed men – about a hundred yeomen under charge of a magistrate – entered and searched it. They were at first gentle and reluctant since many were neighbours and the Yate family was well liked. The atmosphere changed when the sheriff's man George Eliot joined them, armed with a warrant from Wantage. Frizer was with him. Eliot reinforced the yeomen with soldiers, urging them into every chamber, upending beds and furniture and banging on the walls with their hilts and shafts for sounds of hollowness within. But they found not the hair of a priest, and the magistrate, Justice Fettiplace who had accompanied them, apologised most graciously to Mrs Yate, making plain his relief at finding nothing.

But Eliot was not satisfied. He stood in the middle of the drawbridge with Frizer to prevent anyone leaving. In a loud voice he read a passage from his warrant which ordered searchers to make holes in internal walls and take up floorboards. One, a local man who could read, stood looking over his shoulder and objected that there was no such passage. Eliot ordered Frizer to have the man arrested as a Jesuit sympathiser and threatened ruin to Justice Fettiplace if he did not order another search. Fettiplace agreed on condition the man was released, which was done, and another search began, provoking Mrs Yate to wailing and weeping. After much destruction and while it was still going on, she took ill and begged she might be allowed to sleep. Justice Fettiplace agreed and she had a bed made up in an attic that had already been searched. A sentry was placed at the bottom of the stairs.

Christopher witnessed all this with his own eyes, as well as much of what followed, since he had cleverly connived with Mrs Yate and the cook to produce food and drink to mollify the weary searchers. He took it on trays to wherever the searchers were, so saw much of what was going on. Frizer, he said, put himself about everywhere, upstairs and down, goading men on, saying, 'We know he's here, I've seen him with my own eyes, we'll find the Papist snake if we have to take the house apart. Not a mouse, not a rat will escape us.' When Christopher politely offered him sustenance from his tray Frizer said gruffly, 'I thought you'd be gone.'

'I am with you always,' Christopher replied quietly, making free with the words of Our Lord. He smiled when he told me this, saying it gave him as much pleasure to tease Frizer as to strike him.

They searched well into the night. The hammering and banging did not keep Jane Yate from her slumber, however, and gradually the noise ceased as the searchers wearied and the ale took effect. There were not enough candles to go round and many simply lay snoring on the floor where lack of light had stopped them searching. But not Christopher. He was suspicious that Mrs Yate had chosen to sleep in an attic room normally used by servants. Why should she not use her own? When most of the house was asleep he crept out of the kitchen and up to the attic stairs. The sentry was slumped at the bottom, his back against the wall and his head on his shoulder. Christopher stepped over his legs and carried on up the stairs, stopping at the door to the attic. There were voices within, low and male. He could not distinguish the words but from the rhythm he judged they were praying together. At the end he heard the Amen, then Jane Yate's voice.

There was a pause, followed by sounds of movement and a murmured conversation. As his ear became attuned he recognised Campion's voice from having heard him preach. There were also the voices of two other priests, one urging that they should leave now while the house was in slumber. The other asked whether there were still guards outside. Mrs Yate said they should stay, that this attic had been searched before and their hole undiscovered, they would be safer here and could leave when all the searchers had gone. Campion agreed.

Christopher crept back down the stairs and felt his way through the dark house to find Frizer, who was sleeping on the kitchen floor, across the door. I can recall for you exactly what he said to me, his very words even after these many years. He said: 'I stood by Frizer's sleeping body, making up my mind. I had in my hands the power of life and death. I could wake him and tell him and the fugitives would be found and executed. Or I could say nothing and they would probably escape. I hesitated long, waiting to see whether I cared. And I concluded I cared little whether they lived or died. I was indifferent. Does that shock you, Thomas? Some would say I should have shown mercy to a good man, others that I should have rejoiced at unearthing the fox. I liked Father Campion, a powerful and compelling preacher. Yet I remained indifferent. What does that say about me, do you think? For a long time – well, a minute or so – I stood still, waiting to hear how my heart spoke, whether my heart should sway my mind. But I heard nothing. Feelings are poor guides. Thoughts alone should guide us. And thought told me that these men would force us back to the old religion, with all its priests and Popery, its sale of relics, its superstitions, its wine-is-blood and bread-is-flesh magic, its laws and tithes, and foreign rule. Foreign rule, that was the thing. That would not do. Yet still I hesitated, feeling what it is like to exercise power.'

To me, that last sentence is telling. He saw it not as his duty to his country and the rightful worship of God but as a kind of game, a game of dalliance with himself. Years later he told me that the making of his characters and plays was the nearest he came to that early exercise of the power of life and death. But doing it in his plays was more interesting than the reality of that occasion. 'Reality lacks reality,' he said more than once in later years, 'until it is imagined.'

At that time I was encouraged by what he said because it meant he had no secret longings to return us to papal rule. We could trust him. Of course, it did not follow that he was therefore of the Godly party, like me and Mr Secretary and those we worked with. Indeed, it did not follow that he was of any party – or perhaps it did follow that he was of no party. But I was not troubled about that in those days.

The rest of the story has little to do with Christopher. He roused Frizer who roused George Eliot who called for men and a smith's hammer. They clumped upstairs to Mrs Yate's attic chamber and accused her of hiding the priests. She protested and denied it, then wept when one of the men swung the hammer against the wooden partition behind her bed. It yielded and there, lying together in a dark narrow cell, lay Campion and the other two priests. They were brought out as dawn was breaking.

Christopher did not witness the unearthing, wisely choosing not to associate himself with the discovery. The arrested men were roped together and brought down and the sheriff sent for. Jane Yate was not arrested despite her crime, nor were any of the nuns who were surely complicit. But some of the other men in the house were, including an unsuspecting priest who happened to call that morning. Christopher slipped away, taking advantage of the fact that the young, like the old, are often little regarded.

The prisoners were held for days in the house in reasonable comfort, with Campion even allowed place of honour at the table so that he could hold forth. Eliot and Frizer stayed with them – I never knew Frizer absent himself from free food and drink – and it was reported that Eliot rashly challenged Campion to theological argument. He was confounded when Campion worsted him, graciously forgave him, drank to him and promised to absolve him if he confessed and repented, provided he paid a large penance. I never heard which of those conditions most deterred the sheriff's man.

But everything changed when orders from the Privy Council reached the house. The prisoners were placed under close arrest and taken to London on horseback, their elbows roped behind them, their wrists before them and their feet tied beneath their horses' bellies. In this manner were they paraded through the city to the Tower. A note was pinned to Campion's hat, inscribed, 'Campion, the seditious Jesuit'.

Christopher and I saw them, briefly. I was bidden to take him to Mr Secretary's house in Seething Lane to be thanked and paid for his work. There was a great throng in the streets, with much shouting at the prisoners and merriment at their expense. We could only just see them above the heads of the crowd, bent and weary on their horses. More than once Campion almost toppled and had to be pushed upright by the soldiers.

'No more preaching for him now,' I said to Christopher.

'I'd give my thirty pieces to hear him again. He speaks so well.'

'Just as well you won't, then. He might have persuaded you.'

'He wouldn't do that, but will he live? Might he be spared?'

'No. He preached sedition. He would have had Her Majesty murdered.'

'All in the name of God.' He nodded as if agreeing with something I had said. 'Yet not evil. Just wrong, almost admirably wrong.'

'You don't regret what you did?'

He shrugged. 'Not yet.'

Christopher was in Cambridge during the months of Campion's confinement and racking. Thus he did not hear the public debates Campion was permitted with the deans of Westminster and St Paul's. Some said afterwards that if he had repented on those occasions he might yet have saved himself, though I doubt it. Anyway, he preferred a martyr's death. I saw him hanged, drawn and quartered at Tyburn on the first of December that year. He died as well as a man may in that manner. When the executioner burned the offal I saw his kidney sizzling in the ashes and gave a boy a penny to pluck it out. I have it still on my desk at home, as hard as a nut.

CHAPTER FOUR

I cannot tell you much about Christopher's life during the next few years. I saw little of him. He was in Cambridge and I in London or France. He was one of what Mr Secretary called our pigeons, occasional couriers whom we trusted with confidential letters. They had no idea of the contents nor sometimes of the identities of recipients unless they were well-known gentlemen such as ambassadors. Christopher travelled to Antwerp for us at least once, as well as to Paris. It was one of the letters he brought from Paris in 1586 that ignited the powder train culminating in the execution of Mary, Queen of Scots, though he had no idea of it at the time. Nor later, I suspect. Agents often never know the parts they play.

Our quarry then was Thomas Morgan, Mary's chief intelligencer, a Welshman living and plotting in Paris. He was determined to put Mary on the throne of England. Mary, of course, had been held here for many years following her flight from Scotland amid mayhem and tales of murder. But surely, sir, King James must know his mother's history as well as any man can? He would not wish me to rehearse for him the details of her end?

Very well, in outline. Morgan and Mary maintained a secret correspondence which it was our daily endeavour to intercept. But we were having little luck laying our hands on any of it. Her living and breathing here was as a stone in the national bladder, as Mr Secretary put it, a rival who threatened not only our Queen but our Protestant settlement. As a Catholic who had been nourished in the French Court she had no love for England. Nor was she wanted in Scotland, which was rightfully hers, but men like Morgan worked to persuade her that England too was rightfully hers if only her usurping cousin Elizabeth could be removed. Whether she willed it or no – and, to be frank with you, I suspect she did not at first will it as she did later, when tossed upon the seas of misfortune – she became the standard-bearer for Catholic discontent, the focus of hopes and plots. Not all of which she knew about. It was a constant fear of the Privy Council that Queen Elizabeth would be murdered as the Pope had urged, or would sicken and die, for then Mary would take the throne, the French or Spanish would invade and England and the true Godly religion would be done for.

But Thomas Morgan was our immediate quarry, the key to any serious threats. He came from Llantarnam and was very Welsh in speech – in those days I could take him off to the life and was sometimes asked to do so when Mr Secretary was entertaining. Although a Catholic he was made secretary to the Archbishop of York but, not content with privately confessing his creed, he schemed to force it upon the nation and so was removed to the Tower for some years. After release he removed himself to Paris where he continued to plot against Her Majesty. William Parry, the would-be regicide whose trial and execution we had wrought the year before, confessed that Morgan persuaded him to it.

Morgan's secret correspondence with Mary comprised packets of letters delivered to the house of the French ambassador in Salisbury Court, off Fleet Street. They were conveyed thence to Staffordshire where Mary was kept under guard by Sir Amias Paulet, who had been ambassador to Paris. We knew of this traffic but not of what it consisted nor the identities of couriers. Then, towards the end of 1585, Christopher returned to London with letters from Paris, among which was one from an agent of ours, Nicholas Berden. He was one of our best, the son of a London merchant who became a merchant in France and traded in all manner of goods. He was a Catholic but a loyal one, without political or religious ambitions and content to serve Queen Elizabeth as our lawful monarch. He did not wish to see England under foreign rule and reported frequently to me by letter, under various of my cover names, telling us of the aspirations of English Catholics in France who strove to put Mary on the throne. He was a diligent and productive reporter and we saw to it that plentiful trade was sent his way.

The letter delivered by Christopher in early December 1585 was in one of several packets bringing news that Pope Sixtus V had pronounced another excommunication upon

Her Majesty as a bastard heretic schismatic whom it was the duty of any Catholic to murder. The letter told us that this new papal bull was to be smuggled into England by one Gilbert Gifford who would land at Rye under another name and distribute the bill among the underground priesthood here. When Christopher arrived with it I was in Whitehall working on Spanish ciphers and was summoned to receive him downstairs. He was tired, his pale face reddened and roughened by the sea like any sailor's. He had boarded a boat for Dover but the winds were contrary and they were buffeted days and nights before finally making landfall at Rye.

'I should not be sorry never to go to sea again,' he said.

Had he landed at Dover he would have spent the night at his home in Canterbury but now he felt he should return to Cambridge without seeing his family. The college authorities had already complained about his absences.

'But they remain ignorant of what you are about?'

'Of course. They wouldn't complain otherwise.'

I suggested he rested in Whitehall awhile and then spent the night at Mr Secretary's house. I sent out for food and drink and promised to accompany him there later. Then I retired to open the packets and decode Nicholas Berden's letter. From that, and from a note scribbled hastily upon it, I realised that Christopher must have seen the man Gifford in Paris. I went down to him again when he had eaten. We sat on a long bench away from others where we could talk privately.

'Where were you when you were given the packets by the man you met?' He did not know Berden's name.

'Behind Notre Dame, on the point of the island, as instructed.'

'What did he say?'

'The same as last time: "Greetings, Mr Noakes, what brings you here?" And I say, "I seek food for thought." And he says, "In that case, I have some sweetmeats for you." That is supposed to signify that neither of us suspects we are being watched.' He shrugged. 'Doesn't mean we weren't, of course.'

'He said nothing else?'

'No. Well, not then.' He yawned and scratched his stubble. 'We walked for a while by the river, speaking of trade as if we were in business together. Except that when we passed a stall selling fruit he told me to look well at a man buying some. "You may see that man when you sail," he said. "Have nothing to do with him." When I asked why he said, "I may not tell you but if you hear him say his name, report it when you deliver your letters. But do not speak to him yourself."'

'Did you hear his name?'

'No. We didn't travel together. He wasn't on the boat. I never saw him again.'

'Would you know him if you saw him?'

'Oh yes.' His gaze focused as if on a painting on the wall opposite. 'He has curls, fair curls, and blue eyes.'

This glimpse of Christopher's meant that his return to college was further delayed. When I reported it to Sir Francis he despatched a rider to Rye forthwith with orders that any man of Gifford's description landing from France should be detained. He then ordered that I should post to Rye with

Christopher the next morning to identify Gifford. We were to wait for up to a week. I was not best pleased by this for I had had my fill of travel and a hectic journey through the heavy clinging clay of Sussex tracks was not to my liking. Sometimes it was quicker to take ship down the Thames and round the coast, but not with the winds we had then. Nor was Christopher best pleased to retrace the steps he had so recently and wearily made. But there was no gainsaying Mr Secretary.

The journey was long, wet and wearing. We stayed the night in a wretched inn south of Tonbridge where the fleas persecuted us mightily. It was better when we reached Rye and put up at the Mermaid, a commodious establishment serving plentiful fish and good mutton from the Romney Marsh. The harbourmaster assured us that his searchers had been alerted to look for anyone of Gifford's description but that there had been none on the last two vessels from France, both diverted like Christopher's from Dover. The sea was still surly and the wind fitful; local vessels did not venture far from the shore. We were there two days with nothing to do except to explore the small town, waiting and watching as is so often the way in our profession.

We must have talked a good deal but I am afraid I cannot now recall much of what we said. I do remember that Christopher was always keen to hear of life at Court and of the doings of the great men there. Although I dwelt but in the suburbs of that world, I knew some of its denizens and heard much about it from casual gossip. I'm sure he also spoke about Ovid and probably about his own ambitions in poetry and theatre, but I recall nothing of it.

Actors, you say? Actors he was fond of? Did he mention any? Not that I recall.

Anyway, late afternoon on the second day we heard there was a ship sighted off the harbour mouth. We hurried down to the quay and saw a vessel labouring in heavy seas, making slow progress. One of the searchers recognised it as a French vessel out of Rouen. When it finally made it to the quay we stood back among the tall net huts to watch the people come ashore. Some poor souls could barely walk and had to be helped, all the others were unsteady on their legs, staggering like drunken men. They looked exhausted and a few simply sat on their bundles, heads bowed between their knees until they found strength to offer thanks to God for their deliverance. Among the first to recover was a tall man with curly fair hair and a short beard.

Christopher touched my arm. 'That's him, that's your man.'

I gave the word to one of the searchers and we hid behind the netting sheds while Gifford was arrested. He was to be taken under military guard to London for interrogation. Our task accomplished, we left the soldiers to it and spent a final night in the Mermaid, with a fine mutton pie. I do remember what we talked about during that dinner, however.

It began with him saying, 'Can you remember why Judas did it?'

He spoke as if we'd just been discussing Judas. But we hadn't, not since Christopher's mention of him at the time of the Lyford Grange affair. 'Of course. For thirty pieces of silver.'

He shook his head. 'You're no better than the Papists, you don't know your Bible. You should study more. Do you not recall what Mark says? He says that while Jesus and the disciples sat at meat at the house of Simon the leper a woman came and anointed Jesus with spikenard, a very precious ointment. And the disciples were indignant at the waste, pointing out that the ointment could have been sold and the money given to the poor. But Jesus rebuked them, saying, "For ye have the poor with you always, and whensoever ye will ye may do them good; but me ye have not always." Immediately after that Judas went to the Pharisees and offered up Jesus. He accepted the thirty pieces of silver they give him but clearly that's not really why he did it. He did it because of Jesus's self-aggrandisement, His intoxication with Himself and His mission, contrary to the message He had been preaching about relieving suffering and helping the poor. Contrary, too, to His insistence on poverty for His disciples, that they must give up all they have to follow Him. He had grown above Himself. He was becoming a Caesar.'

Blasphemy shocked me in those days. I urged him to quieten himself lest we both find ourselves at the stake. It was especially shocking that he smiled, as if it were all a joke. But he would not be quiet. 'Then, of course, Judas betrayed him with a kiss, he was seized and as he was taken away a young man followed, wearing only a linen cloth. They seized him too but he escaped and ran away naked, leaving his linen cloth behind. Unlike our man today, who had no such enthusiastic followers and no chance to run away, thanks to us. What do you think these details mean, why does Mark give them?' He drank his beer, keeping his eyes on mine.

'I don't know. Anyway, Judas hanged himself.'

'Indeed he did. But only after returning the money. What does that tell us?'

'That he felt guilty.'

'For betraying his friend or for taking money for it?'

'Both, surely.'

'And what if he hadn't felt guilty? What would he have done then?'

'Kept the money and spent it.'

'In which case he'd have deserved to hang, having betrayed Jesus for his own greed. But it wasn't greed, was it? He returned the money. The reason he betrayed Jesus was surely Jesus's own self-aggrandisement.'

'You should be a preacher, Christopher. But you couldn't preach that. You'd be burned for it.'

He smiled again. 'You wouldn't like anything I'd preach. No one would.'

I was troubled by that. I had inklings of what he was getting at, of course, but openly free-thinking, atheistical speculation was something I had never encountered. Heresies I knew about, and various perversions of the gospel truth, but this was different. It continued to trouble me and during our long ride back to London I spoke of it again. 'You seem obsessed by Judas. Do you fear that in what you do for us you resemble him? Even though you agree that we rightly protect the true Godly religion and the security of the state? You don't disagree with that?'

'But that's just how Judas would have thought, minus the security of the state. He must have thought he was acting to save the true Godly religion. He'd have said he joined the movement to help the poor, which is true to Old Testament teaching, and because he believed Jesus when He said that heaven was at hand. Instead of which He who proclaimed Himself the Son of God was now betraying the poor through His extravagance and self-glorification.'

'But something must trouble you about Judas. You mention him often.'

We were approaching Sevenoaks and the chimneys of the great house of Knole had just come into view. 'What troubles me is not that people might compare me with Judas,' he said. 'I doubt the comparison occurs to anyone but me and even I don't find it close enough to worry about. Unless I've betrayed Jesus without knowing it?' He shook his head and continued slowly. 'No, what troubles me is something closer to home, something of myself.'

'What?'

'What's that?'

We stopped. We had almost crested the wooded hill leading up to Sevenoaks when from the trees to our right came a sudden wailing, a girl's voice begging and pleading. There was a track leading into the trees and Christopher, without waiting for me, prodded his horse along it. I followed and soon we rounded a bend to see a rough-looking fellow wearing a torn jerkin dragging a young girl by her hair. She stumbled behind him, bent low, fighting, struggling and screaming, clutching alternately at her hair and at passing bushes and branches. She had dirty bare feet and wore sackcloth that had seen better days. The only word I could make out from her screaming was 'home', which she kept repeating. Christopher halted his horse, handed the reins to me and leapt from it, making for the man. As he ran he hitched his knife from the back of his belt to the front.

Seeing us, the man stopped and turned, still holding the girl by her long brown hair. She had quietened but remained bent double because of the way he held her.

'Let go of her!' Christopher shouted, his voice echoing in the wooded stillness. The man shouted something back but I couldn't tell what. Christopher stopped running about ten yards from the man, walked slowly up to him as if to parley and then struck him full in the face. The man let go of the girl's hair and staggered back, shocked and disbelieving, bleeding profusely from the nose. He stared for a moment, then turned and ran and was quickly out of sight in the trees. Christopher did not give chase but stood looking after him.

The girl dropped to her knees when the man let go of her hair, the sackcloth riding up over her great bare buttocks. Then she too got up and fled without a word. As she brushed past my horse I glimpsed a round, foolish dirty face with the wide loose-lipped mouth and staring eyes of a village idiot.

We had no more of Judas on that journey. We discussed the

incident, whether the man was abducting the girl or whether he was a father dragging his wayward daughter home. Christopher hadn't thought of that. 'He looked a villain,' he said. 'That's why I didn't wait to parley with him.'

'You looked as if you enjoy a fight.'

'I do. I am not a big enough man to seek a fight but I enjoy it when it comes.'

'What do you enjoy about it?'

'The infliction of justified pain.' He glanced at me. 'And you? I imagine you don't like to fight?'

'My build does not incline me to brawling.'

'You are wiser perhaps than me, Thomas.'

He was paid what he insisted on calling his thirty pieces when we reached London. He then made his way to Cambridge, where doubtless he had to give the authorities some excuse for his absence. It was a lapse on my part not to have thought of that. We should have concocted an explanation that would have satisfied them. There would then have been no need for the Privy Council's letter, with which you will recall I began this long account. It is no excuse to say you cannot think of everything when, in considering the security of intelligence agents, it is your responsibility to think of everything.

Which is what I am trying to do now, sir, at the risk of being long-winded and tedious. I know His Majesty has little love for me for my part in the death of his mother, but I hope he will appreciate that I am doing my best to fulfil his commandment? I hope, too, that he will appreciate that although

Christopher Marlowe had a part in that business he never saw the full picture, at least not until the end. If that is the reason for His Majesty's interest, I can assure him now of that.

And of course it was precisely that, the entrapment of the Queen of Scots, that was keeping us so busy in London at that time. Her secret aspirations and the machinations of her supporters, which led her to the executioner's block and them to their eviscerations, must be well known to His Majesty. But I hope he will forgive me for describing a couple of episodes from those hectic months as they involved Christopher. His role was peripheral but significant, perhaps as much to his own life and death as to the Queen's.

CHAPTER FIVE

Like much that followed, Christopher's further role began
with Mr Secretary's recruitment of Gilbert Gifford, the courier we arrested at Rye. Gilbert, as I came to know him during
the close association we formed, was naturally fearful when
taken to London under escort, expecting gaol and torture.
He was therefore surprised and relieved to be taken to Mr
Secretary's house in Seething Lane, treated as a welcome
guest, given food and wine and a room of his own. He was
guarded, of course, but with such discretion that I doubt he
was aware that every exit from the house was watched and
his every movement within it observed. He was permitted
to rest for most of a day and all night without any questions
put to him, having been told only that Mr Secretary would
be pleased to speak to him when he recovered from his
exhausting journey.

That interview took place the next morning in the larger
study, the one with the globe and other furnishings indicat-
ing Mr Secretary's knowledge, learning and wide interests.
I was summoned to take notes, Francis Mylles, the private

secretary, being otherwise engaged. Gilbert was shown in by one of the blue-liveried servants while another served us all with plum brandy and cake. Mr Secretary rose from his desk and greeted Gilbert almost as an old friend, asking after his journey, hoping he had slept well and suggesting we all sat at the table to the side. He introduced me as his assistant, adding, 'It is with Thomas that you will deal, provided we can all agree on how to further this matter.' Then, while we ate and drank, he spoke no more of business but questioned Gilbert about the prices of goods in Paris, the state of the streets and the mood of the people. By the time we came to business, answering further questions must have felt to Gilbert like a natural continuation of the discussion. There was no hint, let alone threat, of the rack. But it was a silent presence above, behind and beneath the conversation. Gilbert did not need reminding of that.

Mr Secretary's manner was polite and serious, his questions precise. Whenever Gilbert hesitated Mr Secretary did not, like most interrogators, repeat the question in different ways, as if nervous of no response or fearing the prisoner did not understand. He simply waited, saying nothing, his hands folded before him. His questions were single aimed shots, clear, direct, factual, impossible not to understand. He never raised his voice but his careful enunciation compelled attention. During those pauses his dark eyes would stare unblinking at the man before him, the silence heavy with unspoken threat.

With Gilbert, I am happy to say, there were few such

silences. He was a loyal and patriotic Catholic, truly horrified when shown evidence that Morgan and his friends were plotting to murder our lawful queen and impose foreign rule. He had agreed to become Morgan's clandestine courier and had learned the art of secret writing in order, he believed, to keep the flame of Catholicism alight for the day when England should return gratefully to the old faith. But he was no assassin. Also, he was a young man of gentle upbringing still reeling from the shock of arrest, despite his kind treatment. The promise of freedom in return for doing exactly what Morgan had sent him to do, with the sole addition that he should share knowledge of it with us, weighed heavily with him. Yet he hesitated. He sympathised, he said, but was finding it difficult to agree. It was a big step.

With many agents the offer of money would have shortened the step and I expected Mr Secretary to broach this delicate but usually welcome subject. 'Is it a problem of conscience, Mr Gifford?' he asked.

Gilbert looked from one to the other of us. 'It is, sir, but not because I disagree with your moral reasoning.'

There was another silence. Then Mr Secretary, speaking quietly, said, 'Your father, perhaps?'

Gilbert's fresh face opened with relief. 'Yes, sir, my father as you must know suffers for his Catholic beliefs. He suffers in his person, too.'

'Aye, and in his purse.' Mr Secretary nodded. 'He has been fined and gaoled for propagating the Pope's cause. And he languishes in prison now, unwell, I hear.'

'He is indeed very sick, sir. I wanted to visit him only Thomas Morgan forbade me because it would draw attention to my presence here.'

I expected Mr Secretary to offer to arrange a discreet visit but he went farther. 'Such filial concern speaks well of you, sir. Would you like me to enquire whether the Privy Council might order his release so that he could take the waters for his health and even perhaps return to his house in Staffordshire? On condition, of course, that he worships only in private and neither practises nor propagates the Pope's cause in public?'

Gilbert nodded vigorously. 'I would, sir, and I should be most grateful.'

'It shall be done. Thomas, take note. Now let us discuss the arrangements Thomas Morgan made with you.'

And so it was that Thomas Morgan's most secret courier of messages between himself and the Queen of Scots became our man before a single message was passed. Morgan had instructed Gilbert to call on the French ambassador in London and collect the earlier messages to the Queen he was safeguarding there until there was a secure way to deliver them. Gilbert himself was then to find a way to get them to her in Chartley, Staffordshire, where she was held. Then he was to secretly convey her replies to the ambassador in London. We knew from other sources that although some letters had got through the ambassador was sitting on a great many and was waiting for someone to make contact.

'Morgan gave me no idea how to get them to the Queen,'

Gilbert told Mr Secretary. 'I have to find a way myself, which will not be easy.'

'Chartley is in Staffordshire. If your father returns to his Staffordshire house you will have reason to visit the county. Getting messages in and out of the house at Chartley without anyone knowing is something we shall devise together. Meanwhile, it is important that you are known to be a free man. Morgan will have spies in Rye, as in other ports, and may already know of your arrest. Searchers at ports are easily bought, alas. I shall arrange it so that he hears that you were taken to London and briefly confined, along with other travellers recently arrested, because we suspected that priests were being smuggled in. But you convinced us of your innocence and you were released, along with others. Under no circumstances – ever – should Morgan or anyone else know that you have met me.'

And so it was done. Morgan heard of Gilbert's release from that other loyal and useful Catholic gentleman, Robert Poley. When in Paris Poley moved in émigré circles and had contrived an introduction to Morgan. Typically, he so endeared himself that Morgan recruited him. Except that Poley's role was not to convey messages like Gilbert but to help coordinate a group of Catholic gentlemen in England who planned to put Mary on the throne. That group was, of course, young Master Babington and his friends, led by Father Ballard. But that was not the only way the ever-helpful Poley made himself useful to Morgan. He had good contacts in Scotland and knew discreet ways to them. Morgan planned to call on Scottish aid against the English in the event of civil war. Thus were we kept informed of Morgan's Scottish plans and contacts. But His Majesty must surely know all this?

Well, sir, that was not all. Morgan had a spy in the household of Sir Philip Sidney, then the most admired and influential soldier and courtier, husband of Mr Secretary's beloved only daughter, Lady Frances. We did not know about this spy until Morgan told Poley about him because he wanted the spy to introduce Poley into the household. His plan was that Poley would report what the well-informed Sir Philip would say privately about Privy Council matters. With the blessing of Sir Philip and Lady Frances, the spy was allowed to remain in place until he had introduced Poley. What Poley then reported back to Morgan was, of course, only what Mr Secretary wanted Morgan to believe.

And so by God's grace, by luck and by our own calculation, we had in Nicholas Berden, Gilbert Gifford and Robert Poley three men who not only knew our enemy's intimate thoughts but could influence and guide them. Also, here at home we had the services of Maliverey Catilyn, an agreeable gentleman welcome in every important Catholic household in England. He was even more welcome in Seething Lane for the descriptions, observations and names which he reported during his weekly nocturnal visits.

The next few months were the busiest in all my time serving the security of the state. Work grew before my eyes, with every day more letters, more facts to be sifted and recorded and more cipher work, the latter greatly increased thanks to

Nicholas Berden. So trusted was Nicholas by the scheming émigrés in Paris that they gave him the alphabets, as we call them, the keys to their ciphers. This meant that I could find ways in that would otherwise have taken months of trial and error. It meant too that I wasted no time on nulls, meaningless symbols and figures placed to delay and confuse. And since success breeds success I could therefore decipher ever more, so creating for myself yet more to read and do. I remember particularly that winter evening when Gilbert Gifford was shown into the little private room in Whitehall Palace bearing twenty-one packets handed to him by the French ambassador for Queen Mary. They were the accumulated secret correspondence of many months which the ambassador had no way of communicating until Gilbert arrived. Naturally, they had all to be secretly opened, copied and resealed before being sent on their way, leaving me to labour at decryption. I worked days and nights on those packets.

I tell you all this, sir – sparing you much detail – so that you may understand how small a part Christopher Marlowe played in my life at that time. And I in his. I neither went to the playhouses nor sought the latest poems at the printer's by St Paul's. Others did – including Sir Francis – and I acknowledge now that my understanding might have been deepened by it. Indeed, Christopher himself urged me that it would enrich my soul to heed the music of words and feel the impress of other men's minds. But work at that time consumed me entirely and though I loved to hear him speak of such matters, and of the dramas that became his life, I never sought to broaden myself as he, I now see, sought to broaden me.

Why he bothered with me I cannot say, being unable to see myself as I was then, from outside. I was fond of him, as I think he was of me, and during times together when business was not pressing he was curious to probe my mind, asking questions I had never asked myself. Despite his proclivity for violence in word or deed when he felt truth or justice were challenged – to be plain, his readiness for a fight – there was a gentleness in Christopher, a quiet and surprising perceptiveness that showed he sometimes saw through other men's eyes more than they saw themselves.

Once, when he arrived in Whitehall Palace with letters from Holland and I procured ale and bread and we sat talking on a bench, he asked me about my own background – my mother and sisters, my father, my time at Cambridge, our business in the custom house, how I came to work for Mr Secretary. I was explaining when he put his hand on my arm. 'Have you always been afraid, Thomas?'

I was nonplussed. 'Afraid? Afraid of what?'

'Of life, of everything. Of letting go of God's hand?'

I protested I didn't understand what he meant. I was as fearful of God as any Christian should be, but I loved Him and was faithful to Him and trusted in His mercy to be united with Him in the life to come. But even as I protested I sensed Christopher was right: I had always been afraid. I had called it Duty.

Christopher shook his head as I spoke. 'You always speak

as if you feel you were born into debt, born owing. Have you never thought that there is no need to be forever owing to your father, to Mr Secretary, to God? Do you not think that perhaps God would like you to let go of His hand, to take steps on your own and find your own way, like a mother with her toddler? There is a world beyond your duties, Thomas. A life.'

Yet he continued participating in my world, the world of duties, whenever asked. I think it interested him, not only in itself and because of its influence on affairs of state – and because of the cause – but because he liked to test himself against it. There was something unresolved in Christopher, a bundle of contradictions which I think he sought to unpick in his work for us and – judging by how he used to speak of them – in his plays. My reaction to anything I feared was to avoid it, but he rushed at it and embraced it. Or so it seemed.

His greatest fears? I cannot say, sir. He never spoke of them to me in those terms but he did once say that in his plays he confronted what in himself he could not. He said something similar about his work for us: 'In my work for you I am an actor. I speak your lines and thereby learn what it is like to be such a man.' Indeed, he made a small but significant contribution to the business I was describing, the plot by young Babington and his friends to murder Queen Elizabeth and put the Queen of Scots on the throne. Although he was on the periphery of this great matter, he did play small parts, twice and briefly.

The first occasion followed from the delivery to Queen

Mary of Gilbert's twenty-one packets. Gilbert, posing at our suggestion as an apothecary, journeyed to Chartley and was received by Queen Mary's private secretary for English affairs, a man called Curll. Gilbert told the guards at the moat that he was an apothecary authorised by the Court in London to provide the Queen with a list of herbs attainable in England to treat the various ailments she suffered. He was instructed, he said, to show the list first to Sir Amias Paulet, under whose charge she was. The guards sent a message to Sir Amias, who – discreetly primed by us – acknowledged that he was expecting this, said he was busy and ordered Curll to see to Gilbert.

Sir Amias was, of course, well primed for his part in this theatre. He was privy to all our machinations because we had to circumvent the very measures he put in place to guard the Queen and monitor all she did. But Curll knew nothing of it, of course. Gilbert was received by him, showed him the enciphered messages he had from Morgan which vouched for him as messenger, and passed him the packets of letters. He also gave him the list of herbs that was cover for his visit, saying he must be sure to show it to Sir Amias. Thus were Gilbert's bona fides accepted and regular communications established.

But since it would be implausible for Gilbert to appear too often at Chartley under his apothecary's cover, we had to find intermediaries who could be sent as messengers from him. So far as Curll was concerned, they did not know what they were delivering along with their herbs. Indeed, when we first did this the messenger genuinely did not know. He was one Barnes, cousin to Gilbert and a known and trusted Catholic, but he proved unreliable and disappeared back to France. Perhaps he suspected he was being used in ways he could not fathom.

We therefore sought people who knew what they were doing and whom we could trust. I suggested Christopher because he had some experience, was always anxious to earn more money and could be summoned from Cambridge at short notice.

He and I rode together to Burton-upon-Trent, near Chartley, where we were to stay at the inn and I was to introduce him to Gilbert. I remember little of the journey and almost nothing of what we talked about, though we must have talked much. There was probably something of Cambridge and of his play and poetry-making and inevitably something of Ovid. I could not for obvious reasons talk much of my own work, apart from the role he was to perform. I must have said something of myself, though, because I remember him turning in his saddle with a smile and saying, 'Why do you want to marry? Because it is ordained? Or for purposes of increase?'

I said I would like a wife to be my companion and keep house for me and keep me warm at night.

'You could hire a woman for that. You don't need to marry. There are plenty who would keep you warm at night without benefit of clergy.'

It was true that many lived in such manner but I wanted

to do it properly, to be blessed by the state of holy matrimony. I did not want my children to be bastards.

'They're often the interesting ones,' he said.

'And you? You too will surely marry when you can support a wife and children?'

He looked away. 'Matrimony may be a state ordained and blessed by the good Lord but we are not compelled to it, are we? Jesus did not marry. Nor John.'

'Do you not wish for companionship and the comforts of family? Children to support you in your old age?'

'I have never desired increase.'

I remember no more of that conversation but I suspect he spoke truthfully. It is hard to imagine Christopher encumbered with wife and children. He was a solitary flame who burned brightly.

He had twice set eyes upon Gilbert, of course, in Paris and at Rye, but they had not met. When they did they got on well, even, by the end of dinner, teasing each other as if they were college friends. Gilbert had studied at universities in France and Italy and had an enthusiasm for ancient literature as well as philosophy. I had never seen Christopher so animated and understood now why he was popular with his fellow scholars, as I had heard. I felt like a fond father struggling, at times, to keep up. Except when it came to our business, when I had to take charge.

'You must tell Christopher what he should say and what will happen when he is stopped at the Chartley moat,' I told Gilbert. 'And how he should speak to Curll.'

Gilbert leaned forward, elbows on the table, lowering his voice. 'There will be two soldiers on your side of the moat. They are suspicious of strangers. I have herbs prepared you can carry in your bag and you must say you come from me, the apothecary, with herbs for the Queen of Scots to be delivered to the hand of Sir Amias Paulet. Sir Amias will depute Curll to receive them. When you are alone with him you pass Curll the letters I shall give you and receive from him any that the Queen is sending. You must say nothing about them, show no curiosity, act as if your main concern is the herbs and the letters are of no interest, nothing to do with you. Curll knows we have to devise a better means than these calls which already are beginning to attract attention. Last time one of the guards joked about the Queen of Herbs, she has so many now. But do not expect pleasantries from Curll. He is dutiful and wary and afraid of Sir Amias. They all are. He is a zealous guardian and the Queen complains of his harshness.'

I was not surprised to hear that. Having worked with Sir Amias when he was ambassador to Paris I knew him for a punctilious servant to our Queen and a dedicated enemy of the old religion. Like Mr Secretary, he had witnessed the massacres of Protestants in Paris.

Christopher rode out to Chartley the next morning. He was away an unconscionable time and, fearing that something had gone wrong, I eventually rode out myself. Knowing Sir Amias, I could say I had business with him if necessary. As I approached the grounds I met the landlord of our inn coming away with his brewer's dray. He was a great hearty fellow with arms like other men's thighs. His relentless good cheer masked an equally relentless pursuit of money which, along with dog-like devotion to whomsoever had power over him, rendered him trustworthy. Sir Amias had personally approved him as supplier of ale to Queen Mary and her followers and in return for a generous stipend, discreetly handled, he informed Sir Amias of anything he learned. He was forever protesting his honesty, to us and to his customers alike. Following Sir Amias's lead, we referred to him not by name but simply as 'the honest man'.

He knew me only as an occasional traveller who paid promptly but he must have suspected I had some connection with what was going on at Chartley. We exchanged greetings, with me pretending I was out to exercise my horse and he pretended to believe me. I asked as casually as I could if he had seen my travelling companion, who had business at the house.

'The young man with herbs? Yes, sir, I have seen him, waiting his turn like everyone else. It is busy there today, not only me and your herb man but the world and his wife have found reason to call. Sir Amias is in a choler with them all and now the Queen insists she must ride out to breathe the air and he must find soldiers to escort her. It is a great to-do. Ride on and you will see for yourself.'

He flicked his carthorse on. I should have turned back, having learned what I needed to know, but just as curiosity killed the cat, so it spurred me on that day. I had a yen to set eyes on Queen Mary, having heard she was beautiful.

Within a few minutes of riding farther into the grounds I could see the house and the moat through the trees. There was a bustle of people about the drawbridge and I had pulled up, determining to go no closer, when I heard hooves and wheels behind me. A carriage with half a dozen soldiers as outriders approached slowly along a track among the trees to my right. I backed up to make way and as the carriage passed I beheld her.

To those who never set eyes upon the Queen of Scots, I can say that, even at twenty or thirty yards, hers was a face to launch a thousand ships, as our poet put it. Framed by abundant red hair, it had a clarity and a fineness that leapt across distance like a bright light, claiming your attention to the neglect of all else. Hers was an almost unreal glamour which, while you beheld it, eclipsed in your mind those other qualities, moral and personal, that made her so unwelcome in Scotland and such a threat in England.

She stared hard at me and bade her carriage stop. She beckoned and I approached to within a few yards. This was not at all what I had planned and I was uncertain how to proceed.

'Oo are you?' she asked. She spoke English through her nose, like most French. She could not pronounce her H.

'Thomas Phelippes, if please your Majesty.' I had been about to use one of my other names but thought that if she were to make trouble I would have to seek protection from her keeper, Sir Amias, who knew my in my own name.

She stared at me for some moments more, then turned away and bade her carriage continue.

When she passed it was as if the sun had left me and I was back in the shadows in which I normally subsisted, a man of low stature with yellow hair and beard and a face marked with the pox. The sight of that Queen, with her impossible beauty, made me despair of marriage. What hope had I, how would I ever meet a woman who would have me? Yet, while God spared me from age and infirmity, I was still determined to find a good wife. On my ride back to our inn I did not think at all of our great matter.

When Christopher returned that afternoon I told him I had seen the Queen. He had too, he said. She had set off in her carriage while he was waiting to be admitted to Curll.

'Did you not think her beautiful?'

'Yes, she is striking.' He nodded as if contemplating an abstract quality. Then he looked at me. 'A face does it for you, eh, Thomas? A face is enough?'

'A face such as hers, yes.'

He smiled. 'You are too easily smitten.'

He had done his job, passing the letters to Curll and receiving some from him which by candle that night I had to carefully open and set about deciphering, which was never easy work. But it was the next morning that he suggested the ruse, sir, that is the reason I am telling you all this. I had paid our bill and as we waited for our horses to be brought round I remarked on our host's cheerful rapacity. Under cover of banter he had tried to charge for more ale than we had drunk. When I pointed it out he did not argue but laughed as at a joke.

'An honest knave,' said Christopher. 'You know where you are with such men. Who pays him owns him. I helped unload the barrels while I was waiting and they gave me an idea for your future letters. Those barrels. Every week they go into the house and every week others come out. Why could not Queen Mary's secret correspondence go in them? Wrap the letters in something waterproof so that they float in the ale, then Curll could find them and send the Queen's replies in the same manner. Your honest man would surely do it for you in return for some additional consideration.'

Thus was established the system that gave us oversight of all the Queen Mary's correspondence with Thomas Morgan, and with all those in England who plotted the murder of Queen Elizabeth on her behalf. Gilbert called again on the house and suggested the arrangement to Curll, who thought it excellent, Mr Secretary agreed and Sir Amias dropped more silver into the open hands of the honest man. The result was that we knew the intelligence conveyed to her before she did, and read her replies before they reached their recipients. We would have managed without Christopher's ingenious suggestion but it would have been more cumbersome, more vulnerable to discovery, and taken longer.

His second contribution to the great matter was less clear-cut. It occurred later in the summer, by which time we had a comprehensive understanding of what Babington and his fellow plotters intended. Do I really need to describe this to you, sir? It became very well known. His Majesty surely knows it. Unless His Majesty has reason to fear such a plot against himself? Could that be the reason for his interest? If so I—

Very well, Christopher Marlowe's role. But I need to describe the whole to make that clear. Is it possible perhaps that we could order more coals for the fire? And more ale? I thank you, sir, I thank you.

You will know, then, that Queen Mary entered a fateful correspondence with the wealthy and foolish young Babington, a gentleman of Derbyshire who had previously delivered messages from Morgan to the Queen. Now, leaving his wife and children at home and restless for further adventure, he took lodgings in London where he met John Ballard, the priest who pretended to be Captain Fortescue. They had known each other in Paris and Ballard travelled secretly to London, armed as I have said before with the Pope's commission to dispose of the usurper Elizabeth and install Mary on the throne. He recruited Babington, and Babington in turn a number of other young Catholic gentlemen with time on their hands, money in their purses, adventure in their hearts and little in their heads. They were persuaded by Ballard that unless Elizabeth was removed there would either be a massacre of Catholics in England, as there had been of Protestants in France, or Spain and France would jointly invade. Thus, the plot against Elizabeth seemed to them not only a rightful restoration of the old faith but a patriotic duty and a great saving of Christian lives.

In July of that year, 1586, young Babington wrote the letter that eventually caused the Queen to reply in what we called 'the bloody letter', the letter that damned her. In his letter Babington told her that the princes of Europe were preparing 'for the deliverance of our country from the extreme and miserable state wherein it hath too long remained'. I have it by heart, that letter, even after these many years, so familiar did I become through going over my decipherment with Mr Secretary time and again. Babington proposed that England would be invaded, Mary freed and Elizabeth removed: 'the dispatch of the usurper, from the obedience of whom we are by excommunication of her made free, there be six noble gentlemen, who . . . will undertake that tragical execution.' Those words were the plotters' death warrants. But not quite Queen Mary's because it did not absolutely prove her complicity. For that we needed her own words.

Babington wrote the fateful letter in his London lodgings then handed it to one of the anonymous young men who collected correspondence for the Queen of Scots on behalf of the French ambassador, usually without knowing what they were doing. The ambassador would then have the letters secretly conveyed by Gilbert to our honest man in Burton-upon-Trent who would conceal them in the beer barrels for Curll to find. I would meanwhile have copied and deciphered them. Sometimes we intercepted them immediately, as on this occasion when the anonymous young man was provided by us and brought the letter straight to me. Babington was a careless encipherer who made frequent mistakes, which in some ways aided my work and in others slowed it because his errors were meaningless and I had to reconstruct what he must have thought he was saying. When I had finished the copying the original was resealed and sent on its way to Staffordshire.

As I said, that letter was sufficient to hang Babington and Ballard and the other plotters but not enough to hang Queen Mary. We needed an incriminating response, and for that we had to wait. Ten long days we waited. Queen Mary, for all her foolish past conduct, was cautious of commitment and exposure. She wrote nothing in her own hand, not even notes. She would dictate her replies to Curll, who would put her words into cipher and conceal the missive in an ale barrel. On this occasion I was in Staffordshire awaiting it when the honest man, who by now knew my business, retrieved it and handed it to me. Thus was I copying, deciphering and reading Queen Mary's reply long before the original reached young Babington in London.

Curll was a much better encipherer than Babington and, knowing his keys, it took me little more than a day to unlock his work, make a fair plain-text copy for Mr Secretary and send it by rapid despatch. I took the original with me back to London, confident that Babington would know nothing of any delay when eventually he received it from one of the anonymous young men. I wanted Mr Secretary to see it, in case he wished to show it to the Privy Council or even Queen Elizabeth herself, such was its import. The crucial passage was that in which Queen Mary commended Babington for his zeal in combating enemies who sought 'the extirpation of our religion out of this realm with ruin of us all'. She then added ten words which sharpened her executioner's axe, words which showed she acknowledged and accepted the plot to murder Queen Elizabeth: *By what means do the six gentlemen deliberate to proceed?* That was why we called it 'the bloody letter' – we knew blood would run after those words. That the Queen knew well what she was about was further evidenced by her urging Babington to 'fail not to burn this present quickly'.

Once that letter was in Babington's hands we knew we could move against the plotters and finally against Queen Mary herself. But for the latter we needed the authority of Queen Elizabeth. It was well known at Court that she was reluctant to execute a fellow Queen, her cousin at that. Mr Secretary and Lord Burghley found it hard even to discuss it with her.

The Court was at Greenwich when I reached London and I had to go by river to meet Mr Secretary there. He wanted to see the original letter before it was delivered to Babington. He took me to one of the many small rooms of the palace, one that he had made his own by furnishing it with maps and books, although he was not often there. He was in better health this time and greeted me warmly.

'I thank God for you, Thomas. You are truly an instrument of His work. But that does not relieve us of the necessity of continuing to strive to the uttermost in His cause. I think we have more to do with this letter.'

He had on the desk before him the plain text copy I had sent in advance and now laid the enciphered original beside it. He looked from one to the other, stroking the point of his beard with the thumb and forefinger of his left hand. 'It is plain to anyone that the Queen of Scots implicitly acquiesces in this plot to murder her cousin and restore papal rule. It will be plain too that Babington and Ballard and their friends are mired in guilt. But I worry that plainness by implication may not be sufficient for the law to convict her under the Act for the Queen's Surety, which requires proof that she is privy to the conspiracy, that she is engaged in it, is part of it. For that, something else may be needed.'

I doubted we could provoke her into being more open. 'She is cautious. Babington will not seek further authority because he will think he has it in this. And if we delay, the plotters who are now gathering like crows on the threshing floor may fly away and disperse.'

'I know, Thomas, I know.'

He continued to stroke his beard, gazing at the columns for figures in the enciphered letter. Somehow, in those moments of silence that felt like minutes, I began to divine his thoughts. I could hardly bring myself to say what I thought he was thinking, it seemed so great a hazard. But neither could I resist.

'Unless, Mr Secretary, we added words to her letter.'

His dark eyes rested on mine. I felt he had been waiting for me to say it. He nodded. 'It needs a postscript.'

It is curious to relate now, sir, but I may as well confess to you that after these many years I still remember my heart beating faster as I stood before him. What he proposed was a great and dangerous undertaking, the introduction of a forgery into a court of law convened under oath before our Lord. But Mr Secretary was quick to end my hesitation.

'We must be very careful of the phrasing,' he said, 'and you must be very sure of your writing. And it must be done with all speed. We cannot delay delivery much longer.'

I put my reservations aside and we worked on it together for the rest of that day in Greenwich. We had first to agree what should be said, words that made Queen Mary's intention, already implicit in what she had dictated, mortally clear. They had also to be true to her manner of correspondence, bearing in mind that she thought in French and turned it into English. And they had to follow on naturally from what was already written. Once that was agreed, I had to translate it into Curll's cipher, expressing it as he would have while ensuring that Babington would understand it. Then I had to copy Curll's script precisely.

Fortunately, I have since childhood had the happy gift that, shown a man's hand, I can copy it so closely that he himself would think it his. It is the same with any man's voice, accent or mode of speech. This gift of mimicry I never had to cultivate or work at. I simply grew up finding I had it, as some men may naturally and easily catch a ball, and others woo a woman.

Even so, it took time. We had to send for inks like that which Curll had used, then mix them to get the right shade. I tried, shaped, tried again a dozen quills until I had one with which I could repeat his strokes precisely. Then I wrote out the eight lines of cipher three or four times on other paper to ensure I had his script exactly. Finally I added it to his letter. I can tell you now, from memory, how those ciphered columns read:

> *I would be glad to know the names and qualities of the six gentlemen which are to accomplish the designment, for that it may be I shall be able upon knowledge of the parties to give you some further advice necessary to be followed therein; and as also from time to time particularly how you proceed and as soon as you may for the same purpose who be already and how far every one privy hereunto.*

Next it had to be resealed, a demanding task requiring great exactitude for which we used Arthur Gregory, a Dorset man and our master forger. The letter was handed to Anthony Babington the next day by someone he recalled afterwards only as 'a homely serving man in a blue coat'.

I hope you will inform His Majesty, sir, that this postscript, those fatal words Mr Secretary and I put together, was never used against his mother? When the letter – her own alone, the real letter – was read out at her trial it was shorn of that paragraph we forged. She was judged and condemned through her own words entirely. Mr Secretary discussed it with the Privy Council and after much debate they agreed it was better to trust to the words the Queen of Scots herself had dictated than to risk the whole case against her through allegations of forgery. It was not that the forged paragraph said anything she did not believe or wish for but that any doubt about it – she would surely protest it was not hers, as would Curll – might undermine the truth of what she had in fact said. That alone should have been enough to execute her – and was, as proven. I must tell you, sir, I was much relieved.

As for Christopher, I give you this detail so that you may know the context of his dealings with us and understand what his role was and was not. For all his fame as a play-maker, he was never a principal player in our great drama. Yet, as you shall hear, it was through his association with us that he met his end.

While Mr Secretary and I worked on the letter, Anthony Babington gave a great supper for his friends at the Castle tavern in Cornhill. At the same time and at a separate dinner Nicholas Berden, who had come from Paris, was hoping to be introduced to Ballard, the moving spirit of the conspiracy. We had both events covered but Ballard did not turn up – he was in Sussex, it transpired – and anyway Babington had not yet received the incriminating letter, still less had time to act upon it. Time was pressing – delivery of the letter could not be long delayed – but Mr Secretary was determined that we should not move until the trap was set for springing.

He ordered me to his house at Barn Elms two days hence with Robert Poley, Ingram Frizer, Nicholas Skeres and Christopher, if he was still in London. Thus, unknown to any of us, we assembled the full cast of Christopher's death a few years later. I did not know Skeres except by name as someone who worked with Poley and Frizer and, though I had met

Frizer since Christopher's unfortunate introduction to him at Lyford Grange, I could not claim to know him. Poley I knew as well as anyone could know a man who was at all times all things to all men. As well as getting himself recruited by Thomas Morgan he had become the bosom friend of young Babington, nurturing him like the fondest of wet-nurses. They shared lodgings, Poley presenting himself as a trusted intermediary to Mr Secretary. Babington, you see, never knew what he really wanted – he veered between plotting to murder the Queen, desiring to negotiate with her via Mr Secretary for the safety of Catholics in England, or himself fleeing abroad. I suspect he would most have liked the second of these, had it been practical, but the third would have been better for him. Intelligencing is like war, in that anyone lacking sureness of aim pays a price, as Anthony Babington did.

When the letter was finished and delivered I was instructed to find Christopher if he was still in London. If he wasn't, there was no time to get him back from Cambridge. Mr Secretary had not told me why he was required; he had hitherto been kept as a man apart, not mixed with others in our business apart from Gilbert Gifford. But those were busy times. We had watchers and spies everywhere – in and around the French and Spanish embassies, following Babington and his friends, in and around Chartley and watching for Ballard, as well as messengers and couriers speeding throughout the kingdom. Anything of interest had to be reported to Mr Secretary or Francis Mylles or me, then assessed and acted upon. There were watchers too at the

Channel ports, spies in Paris, Rome, Madrid and the Low Countries. Every strand of this great web stretching over all Europe was drawn into the mind of Mr Secretary, the only place where all was known.

Deciphering and translating are silent, sedentary, solitary tasks demanding time and concentration. Our successes created a flood of letters and documents. Journeying to Staffordshire and even downriver to Greenwich were interruptions whose disruptive effect spread well beyond the time they took, since whenever I returned to deciphering I had to rebuild my concentration. Also, I had for that year been made a member of parliament for the port of Hastings in order to vote for government business and therefore had to attend some sessions, though I never went to Hastings. But when I sat at my own desk with a cipher before me I had to empty my mind of all other thoughts and preoccupations. Anything else – from daily bread to worry about my father's business, to what might be happening at Chartley, to where I might find Christopher, even daily prayer – was a distraction. But once I was grappling with a cipher, when I was properly in it and my mathematical imagination engaged, I felt I was in a purer realm. It was as if God had lifted me out of time, purged me of earthly considerations and granted me a glimpse of that truth and beauty of which Plato writes. I do truly believe that the secrets of all the heavens must be mathematical.

I was not pleased, therefore, to begin the day after Greenwich by being bustled and jostled in the streets on my way to find Christopher in the Liberty of Norton Folgate.

He lodged there when in London with Thomas Watson, the famous poet. Watson was a friend of Mr Secretary's and another sometime helper of ours who lived near the theatre called the Curtain, where I believe Christopher's first plays were performed. His house was not easy to find, partly because it was not easy to find a full-witted person who knew anything of his or her own streets and lanes. A woman carrying a capon fled when I stopped her. A young man trembled and stammered and I could get no sense out of him. Others shook their heads or asserted there was no such person in Norton Folgate. None wanted to speak, perhaps because I was wearing Mr Secretary's livery. Eventually I spotted a tall man whose chain of office proclaimed him beadle. He directed me to the house of Widow Turner.

This was a substantial new dwelling with a yard and garden. My knock was answered by a fresh-faced young woman in a plain black dress. No, Mr Watson was not at home, nor Mr Marlowe who shared his room. Both gentlemen had been at home but Mr Watson was out she knew not where and Mr Marlowe had left early this morning, perhaps to return to Cambridge where he mostly lived. But it might be worth asking after him at the theatre which was not far and was where he spent his time when in London. He would be there if not journeying to Cambridge. They both wrote poetry, she added with a smile, and spent as much on candles and ink and paper as most folks on food.

She spoke confidently with a broad West Country burr like Sir Walter Ralegh's, he being a Devon man whom I had heard speak with Mr Secretary several times. She had auburn hair escaping from beneath her cap, large grey-green eyes, pretty regular features and a nice, clear pale skin, marked by freckles but not by the small pox, unlike my own. She also had all her teeth.

Liking her, I encouraged her to talk about the lodgers, reassuring her that I worked for Sir Francis Walsingham, who was a good friend of Mr Watson's. I allowed her to assume it was he I sought. 'But Mr Marlowe is also a lively man,' she added. 'The house is full of gaiety when he is here. They laugh together, so. We all do.'

She sounded as if she had a fondness for Christopher, whose jollier side I had not seen except in his occasional teasing. 'Your mistress also appreciates the company, perhaps,' I said.

She raised her eyebrows. 'My mistress, sir? I thank you but I am sufficient mistress of myself, I hope.'

She was, of course, the Widow Turner. She had maids – two, I discovered, and a cook – but had answered the door herself because she had set them to scrub the floorboards.

In one of his plays or poems – I cannot remember which – Christopher asks, whoever loved that loved not at first sight? I am not sure that that is a universal truth but it was true of me in those few minutes. I wanted to talk further but could think of nothing to say after apologising for mistaking her for her own maid. When I was away from her I conceived all manner of clever remarks to make her laugh or think well of me, but the more I beheld her the more my tongue clove to the roof of my mouth and my mind faltered. I felt no better than the half-wits from whom I had sought directions. All I could do was repeat my apologies, thank her and be on my way. I did not think to leave a message nor even to ask where I could find the Curtain theatre.

But I found it soon enough, the largest building apart from the church. Despite the early hour the place was busy with people, carpenters hammering, sawing and singing, actors shouting and declaiming in their rehearsals. As you know, sir, I had no interest in plays, having no time for them and little liking for the rogues and layabouts they attracted. Not to mention their great danger in plague times. Throughout my childhood the preacher at our church had preached hard against them and I was still not sure that theatres were places for Christians, though it had surprised me to find that Mr Secretary enjoyed the drama. He enjoyed music and painting too, despite being a forward Salvationist opposed to religious compromise. Indeed, as I think I told you, he had helped create one of the acting companies, the Queen's Men. He was also a good friend to Richard Tarlton, the clown. It is possible, of course, that in forming the Queen's Men, who were famous for their plays about our history, he saw them as advancing policy. Mr Secretary was ever mindful of policy.

The man I asked claimed never to have heard of Christopher but a boy nearby asked if I meant Kit Morley. I was accustomed to various versions of his surname but was unaware that among players he was known as Kit. The boy led me to him. He was seated on a bench at the back of the stage behind some scenery on which a hunting scene was half-painted. He was talking to another man of about his own age who had large light-brown eyes and a soft brown beard.

He was surprised to see me, of course, and stood as if for someone important. 'Thomas, greetings, I had not expected you.' He looked slightly awkward but recovered quickly. 'What brings you from Cambridge?'

I had told him not to mix our two worlds but to pretend in public I was a neighbour from Canterbury or knew him at Cambridge. 'Not your play, I fear. Family business of my own. But I come to warn you that there is grumbling among the master and fellows about absences by scholars and yours has been particularly noticed. You must have an explanation when you return.' My invention was unconsciously prophetic, of course.

The other man stood. Christopher made no attempt to introduce him. 'I must go,' the man said. 'The king's speeches, then.' He had an accent I couldn't place.

Christopher laid his hand on the man's shoulder. 'Good luck with that. And I'll look at the other bits.' He watched the man leave, which he did with a nod of acknowledgement to me, then gestured that we should sit.

'You are required,' I told him. 'Mr Secretary holds a council of war tomorrow at Barn Elms. I shall take a boat from Whitehall Palace. You can share it.'

'Why? What for?'

'We are closing the net on them. This end as well as at Chartley.'

'Who else will be there?'

I told him, adding, 'I don't think you'll find your old friend Frizer a problem. He will do as he's told.'

'Who is Skeres? A coney-catcher like the others?'

'I've not met him but Mr Secretary calls on him now and again for small jobs.'

'Like me?'

'I doubt he's like you. And nor would I call Poley a coney-catcher. He's a cut or two above. He wouldn't bother with petty frauds on naive men innocent of London, though he may have started like that. He plays for higher stakes, political matters, Court affairs. But you don't know him either, do you?'

'I met Master Poley in Paris.'

'You never told me.'

'You never asked. He was in high humour, having got himself taken on by Thomas Morgan, as you must know.'

'He told you that?' We tried to avoid our spies knowing each other as spies, unless it was necessary for them to work together. The more they knew the more they could tell if caught and racked. But I had long suspected – and Mr Secretary, I believe, simply assumed – that they discovered and gossiped with each other more than we knew. 'What did you think of Poley?'

Christopher lifted his gaze to the outsized hunting scenery. When in thought his features softened into a vacancy, an abstraction. 'Had he been better born he would have been a courtier, a good one, proud, bold, ready, resolute, who would on occasion stab.'

'You dislike him?'

'Not him, exactly. More myself. I don't much like that of myself I see in him.'

'You see yourself as a courtier, then? One who would stab?'

'Half and half, no more. But that's enough, don't you think? It will serve, it will suffice? I think he sees something of himself in me, too, and is not sure whether to like it. He doesn't trust me.'

'Nor should you him. What is it you think he dislikes in you?'

'Cynicism, Machiavellism, unbelief. I articulate what he embodies, though he knows it not. But he senses it and it makes him uneasy.'

'And you would stab?'

'Of course. Wouldn't you? Isn't that your business? Our business?'

I am somewhat literal-minded and it was not always easy for me to know whether Christopher meant what he said or was teasing for a response. I think I answered that I would not stab unless in fear of my life, always preferring that others did that sort of work for me. If it had to be done.

'Which is as bad as doing it yourself. But such honesty does you credit. I shall speak up for you on Judgement Day. Assuming I am permitted a voice.'

The journey upriver to Barn Elms the following morning took longer than expected because the tide was against us, but our boatman was strong and, what was more, quiet. Christopher and I spoke nothing of our business, of course, but listened to the slap of oars and watched the sun glinting on ripples. We talked a little about plays. He predicted there would be more theatres and more work for play-makers and I recall that he and Watson burned candles in their lodgings at a great rate. Their landlady willingly supplied them, but at a cost.

'I spoke to her,' I said. 'A pleasant woman, a pleasing manner.'

'Mary Turner, a good woman. A widow of two years now.'

'And children?'

'No. Her husband was a printer. He left her comfortable. Comely, too, don't you think?'

I felt awkward about discussing her. Not because I didn't want to – I wanted to talk about her all the time, would happily have accosted strangers with descriptions of her, her very name filled my head with images quite unlike the churchly or saintly reflections it should have engendered. No, my awkwardness was because I recalled the softness of her tone when she mentioned Christopher and I could not believe that he was not at least as attracted to her as I was. And, of course, he could see her daily, or nightly.

Christopher had an aggressive sensitivity which missed little and withheld from little. He saw my awkwardness. 'Stricken by Eros's arrow, are you, Thomas?'

I protested that I had merely remarked her pleasantness and thought she must make a good landlady.

He laughed at that. 'Snared by a wench's glance, eh? A liquid eye and a soft word does it for you? You are a slave to love now. Eros's arrow is barbed, I warn you. There's no plucking it out without pain.'

My protests did not avail. In fact, they provoked further teasing which, to his credit, he ended when he saw I was baffled as to how to respond. 'No, but it is time you took a wife,' he added, sounding more serious. 'You've said it yourself before. Marriage would suit you. You are of the uxorious tribe.'

'And you are not?' I had asked him before, of course, but got no clear answer.

He looked across the rippling water. 'Too much to do. Francis Bacon often says that a man who hath wife and children taken hath hostages to fortune given.'

It was a great relief to me that he had no designs on Mary Turner. If his mind were set on something he would have been a formidable rival.

Mr Secretary's house at Barn Elms was a pleasing spot looking onto a meadow running down to the river. I arranged that our boatman should wait and be refreshed in the kitchen. Mr Secretary did not at first join us, being busy with correspondence. We found the other three already seated at a table in the small orchard and supplied with ale.

His Majesty will not of course have known these gentlemen, though he may have known of Robert Poley. Poley and Skeres must be long dead now. Ingram Frizer is still alive, last I heard. How or where the others died, I do not know, though Skeres probably died in prison. You shall find, sir – if God spares you, as I pray He shall – that age brings not the prosperity and security you hoped but a continuation of youth's troubles and vexations while depriving you of the vigour and means to contest them. Age is unfair.

And if your luck is like mine, sir, you may find you are punished for living into a new reign. Consider that I was once you, as close to the great events of the kingdom as you are now. I was known to great men of the realm such as Sir Francis, Lord Burghley, Lord Leicester, the Earl of Essex, Sir Walter Ralegh and various ambassadors and men of state. My name was known even to the Queen, who once expressed pleasure at my service and rewarded me with a pension. I was privy to secrets and affairs of state that even now would cause men to draw breath.

Yet here I am in the King's Bench prison, ignored, forgotten, discarded like an old shift too often worn. If I am remembered at all it is because some vengeful money-hound pursues me through the courts or because the state harries me for ancient debts to the Crown incurred through youth and inexperience in the last reign. I rot here at the mercy of my enemies, denied work to relieve my debts or to support my beloved Mary who depends upon me. Yet still the state remembers enough of me to demand my old deciphering skills when it suits. If I am still so useful and so trusted with secret matters, may I not at least work from my own house?

And now you, sir, come calling, imploring me to sieve what is left of my memories of a man who died some thirty years ago. You say you may give no reason other than that the King requires it, for why I cannot tell. But His Majesty himself is ailing, you tell me, so I must tell all this day. I pray God relieve His Majesty's suffering and grant him long life. Please assure him of my fealty and say I beg forgiveness for being the only man living to have had a hand in the execution of his mother, which was lawfully done under pressure of circumstances few now comprehend. And tell him I freely confess mis-spent customs dues, buying property with Crown money which I still owe and would repay if I could earn again. And remind him too that Christopher Marlowe was also a man of the old reign, though he at least had the good fortune to die young and quick. He did not live to find himself unknown at Court, recalled only to be used and punished, as if survival is a sin.

Very well, sir, I shall get on, I shall. That day when we all met at Barn Elms was a prefiguring, as I have said, of Christopher's death a few years later. The three present at that fateful occasion were the three whom he and I joined that bright morning in the orchard, including, of course, the man who killed him. I shall describe them for you as best I can.

Ingram Frizer we have met already at Lyford Grange. That gave you the essence of the man: a loyal dog, bullying, robust, hard-riding, hard-dealing. Perhaps no more out for himself than most men but he cared less to hide it and was more successful. He made sure he served his masters well, especially Thomas Walsingham, Sir Francis's nephew whose man he became and whose widow he enriched in diverse dishonest ways, for which he was well rewarded.

You may have heard him described as a bawdy serving-man who argued with Christopher over a wench. That is untrue. He was more than a serving-man, more like a factor or bailiff who ensured obedience to his master's bidding. He was a yeoman, later styled a gentleman. He was never a bawd, no more in drink than most men and taking women only as he found them, not as trade. I believe he later married. Nor do I know of any wench over whom he and Christopher would have argued. It is hard to imagine them having a woman in common.

Nicholas Skeres was a London man, son of a merchant tailor and about the same age as Christopher. He was small and pale with a black beard neatly trimmed and one eye half closed as if frozen in a wink. He studied law at Furnival's Inn, lent money at high rates, bought bonds without paying, when he could get away with it, and sold them to the gullible, who did pay. He was ever in court, suing or being sued. Quiet-spoken and polite, he was a natural deceiver or coney-catcher, on business terms with notorious London street thieves such as Staring Robyn and Welsh Dick. Yet he too styled himself a gentleman and was later servant to the Earl of Essex, whose livery he wore until his master's head was freed from his body. He and Frizer did business together. I heard he died some years ago and, assuming there is more justice in the next world than this, he should now be held to the fire and writhing on the prongs of Satan's fork.

Little more needs saying about Robert Poley than I have told you already save that you needed to feel his charm to comprehend his success. Charm takes you a long way – the earls of Leicester and Essex had it in plenty, both favourites of the old Queen – but if you are to go on rising in the world you need something more. You need luck, judgement and determination. Robert Poley had all three. His was the quiet charm that strokes and calms, making whoever he spoke to feel they had all his attention – as indeed they did, while he wanted something of them. There was nothing brash or declamatory about him, no drawing attention to himself like an actor or clown or those who love to preach. He did not seek to impress you with his own importance, but with yours – at least, with the illusion of it. He had regular features and large grey eyes which twinkled with humour when he had a mind to amuse. Women found him attractive. I believe I mentioned before that while in the gaol during a temporary sojourn on our behalf – it being necessary to preserve his reputation as an enemy of the state – he contrived to seduce a comely goodwife, and may later have married her.

But all the time he hummed with ambition, the ceaseless calculation of his own interests, masked by ease of manner and the balm of plausible lies. Had he not been lowly born he would surely have been a great statesman, an assiduous and successful courtier, as Christopher said. I could imagine him a favourite of the Queen's. Among the few who were not taken in by him were Mr Secretary and – heeding his example – myself, although also Christopher. I have told you already what Christopher said about him. I think he saw straightaway that Poley always carried with him something hidden and I suspect he thought the same of Christopher, because they fenced each other as if in play, neither seeking seriously to stab. But neither letting down his guard. What he thought Christopher might be hiding, I am not sure. I am not sure that he himself would have known, but he sensed something.

A mark of Poley's charm and persuasion was that Anthony Babington, even when fleeing for his life, could not credit how greatly he was betrayed by the man who had shared his room. His farewell to this earth, his very last letter, was written to Poley. He said, 'Robin ... I am ready to endure whatsoever shall be inflicted ... I am the same I always pretended, I pray God you be and ever so remain towards me ... Thine how far thou knowest.' It was never delivered. I found it among his papers when gathering evidence for his trial.

But when we talked in the orchard that morning, amid the dappled sunlight and the buzzing of bees, all this was ahead of us. Men united by common purpose are generally agreeable while things go forward. Christopher and Ingram Frizer greeted each other with rough jocularity, a manner I never saw Christopher deploy with anyone else. Frizer said, 'Aye, we had an encounter in Berkshire, I recall,' to which Christopher responded, 'Followed by an understanding, I trust,' at which they clapped each other on the shoulder like old soldiers reunited.

With Poley Christopher was more circumspect. They nodded and shook hands. 'We met in Paris,' said Christopher, 'and escaped unharmed.'

'So far,' said Poley, smiling.

Christopher and Skeres were introduced, we were offered

ale and all sat to await Mr Secretary. Until he came, which fortunately was not long, we talked of anything but the matter we were gathered for. Poley asked Christopher about the theatre, what was on, who was playing, Skeres and Frizer discussed a court case they were embroiled in, I asked Poley about matters in Scotland, knowing he travelled there on Mr Secretary's behalf. He said that most of the Scottish nobility would be pleased if Mary's head should roll, her presence in England being almost as great a problem for them as for the English. Only the French and Spanish stood to gain by it.

Mr Secretary joined us, striding through the long grass like an avenging angel, dark with purpose. He got down to business immediately, with no preliminaries. 'There are three essentials. Firstly, we must keep the plotters in play so that we may net them when they are all fully committed. They must believe their game is going forward, otherwise they will disperse and we shall lose them. Secondly, we must keep them all under observation in case they decide to act precipitously against Her Majesty, in which case we must be on hand to prevent them. Thirdly, we must catch Ballard the priest – Captain Fortescue as he now calls himself – as soon as possible. Although he may have just joined them – or may be just about to – he is the engine of the plot, the man to make it happen. But he is also the only one we can arrest without compromising it, because priests in hiding can be arrested at any time. We must make his arrest seem like a routine discovery. But first we must find him.'

'He was last heard of in Kent,' said Poley.

'That was days ago. He is on the move but so long as he believes his presence is unknown he is unlikely to flee the kingdom. Where then will he go?' He glanced at us all but resumed too soon for anyone to respond. 'He will go where he can most swiftly bring his plot to a conclusion. He will seek the man best placed to make it happen. Ballard is the trout which will rise to the fly, Babington. Babington is our fly.' He turned to Poley. 'You are still lodging with him?'

'I am, Sir Francis. That is, I was when I left this morning. But he hourly speaks of moving, of running or going abroad, so that I cannot answer for him from one hour to the next.'

Mr Secretary's black eyes rested on Poley's. 'Answer for him you shall. I hold you responsible. He must be here, under our gaze, for Ballard to find. As soon as Ballard is within our grasp we shall arrest him. But we shall not arrest Babington until we can net the whole crew, as I said. They must all be implicated. Even if Babington and Ballard are together the arrest of Ballard must appear a separate matter, with no mention of the plot. Therefore the arresting party will know nothing of it. They will be city officials and royal pursuivants armed with a warrant signed by Lord Admiral Howard. That said, I want our own eyes and ears there when it happens. All three of you' – his glance swept across Poley, Frizer and Skeres – 'are known or suspected of having worked for me. Indeed, it is the prospect of a meeting with me that keeps Babington attached to you, is it not, Mr Poley?'

'He hopes that if he confesses all you will intercede with

the Queen who will in return promise there shall be no persecution of Catholics.'

'You must make sure he continues to believe that. It may be that we shall have to have you arrested, too, in order to deflect suspicion. As a temporary measure, of course.' He turned to Christopher. 'Mr Marlowe, you are not suspected of any association with me so I should be obliged if you would accompany the party to arrest Ballard, whenever it happens. May I trust you to do that?' Mr Secretary often phrased his orders as requests but there was never any doubt as to which they were.

Christopher nodded. He looked pleased.

'Thomas will alert you when it is to happen. You must make sure he knows where to find you at all times. During the arrest you say nothing unless you have to intervene. If Mr Poley is present, as is likely, you will not recognise him. So far as the arresting officers are concerned you are a servant of Lord High Admiral Howard, sent to ensure that the conditions of the warrant are complied with. You will observe Babington and any other conspirators closely and, if necessary, you should assure them that they are not in danger, that it is only the suspected priest you are after.'

The rest of the meeting comprised surveillance instructions for the other three. They were told they were under the command of Francis Mylles and Nicholas Berden, both already deployed on the ground. On our journey back downriver I asked Christopher if he was happy to be involved.

'Grist to the mill.'

'Will you make a play of it?'

'Perhaps. The cause is just and it is an adventure.' He glanced across the water. 'What would I do, what would I not do? How far would any of us go in anything? Do we ever know?'

'You are becoming Narcissus.'

'But we are enjoined to know ourselves, are we not? Except you, Thomas. You do not seek to know yourself. Yourself does not interest you. That is true wisdom, perhaps.' He smiled. 'But you do seek to know the Widow Turner. And now you have reason to call again.'

Chapter Six

That happened sooner than I had thought. One of Lord Admiral Howard's men roused me at my house before dawn the next morning, telling me I was to go to the Rose tavern at Temple Bar. There I would meet others outside the tavern and proceed to Master Poley's lodgings nearby. The man clearly did not know why, nor did he know that it was actually Christopher who was to go there. Ballard must have risen to the Babington fly.

Finding my way to Widow Turner's house in the dark was a hazardous undertaking. The sky lightened as I went, however, and the most fearful thing I witnessed were looming grey figures in the dawn in Holywell Street where some houses had been pulled down for rebuilding. They looked like ghosts assembling and alarmed me at first until I saw they were vagrants who had slept in the ashes of the bonfires to warm themselves. Two were sturdy beggars who made towards me until they saw I wore my sword. There are even more such fires and more new buildings in our city now, are there not, sir? Sometimes I imagine a terrible conflagration. We should be roasted as in the flames of Hell.

It was properly light when I knocked on Widow Turner's door. I expected the servants to answer but eventually she herself called out to know who was there. It was another long wait until she unbolted the door. She wore a shawl and shift, her hair tousled and awry, and before I could explain my mission she began apologising for her appearance, saying she regretted I should see her so untidy. I dared not say I thought she looked most fetching.

She left me to wait in the panelled room while she found a maid to wake Christopher. When she reappeared she kindly offered me bread and sustenance and I was still declining, with genuine regret, when Christopher appeared. He too looked tousled, blinking through the shroud of sleep. I could not explain anything before Widow Turner but merely said we were summoned to our duties. As she closed the door upon us I fancied she gazed almost wistfully, but whether after Christopher or me I could not tell.

I could not participate in the arrest, of course, but walked part of the way with Christopher to Temple Bar, rehearsing what he should say or not say. Before we parted I bought us an apple each from a stall, then left for Whitehall and my numbers and ciphers.

They were ever a solace to me. I accept the necessity of action, of acting in the world, having been obliged to bestir myself more often than I desired. But it always felt like a distraction. A distraction from what? Well might you ask, sir. From the search for truth, from that human quest we find in Plato and the ancients. Now that I am confined here, without my beloved Mary for company, I become more than ever convinced that Plato was right, that truth is to be found in the mathematic. Granted, it is beyond my fathoming, unimaginable, unattainable, but there is in number an echo of eternity that reaches us from beyond the clamour of humanity. I confess I am now more convinced of this than of the truths of scripture which, in those days, I never questioned. Until prompted by Christopher. This may shock you, sir, but if you will have the truth you must hear it. I leave it to you to decide what to tell His Majesty.

Well, he reported to me in Whitehall later that day, after the arrest of Ballard. It went as planned, the other parties to it being a city official and two royal pursuivants. They asked no questions of Christopher, having been told they would be joined by one of the Lord Admiral Howard's men. Armed with clubs, swords and chains, they proceeded directly from the tavern to Poley's lodgings where they found the door unlocked and ajar, though all was dark and quiet within. The explanation for this was that Poley had opened it and was awaiting them, guessing they would come. He whispered that Ballard and Babington were sleeping within, and asked that they knock loudly on the door and that upon his answering they force their way in, handling him a little roughly and perhaps even binding him, but letting him go once they had secured Ballard. They queried this, knowing nothing of Poley or the background, at which point Christopher had to intervene to say that Poley was a trusted man, that they should heed what he said and secure only Ballard, leaving the other one, the young Babington.

Poley quietly closed the door and a minute later the city official banged upon it with his cudgel and demanded entry loudly enough to wake the neighbourhood. Poley opened and the pursuivants barged in, seizing him and demanding to know whether he was the priest, John Ballard. By this time the other two were on their feet in the back room. Christopher could see them crouching, frozen with shock, until Babington suddenly made for the window at the back. But the city official was too quick for him, rushing into the room and thrusting Ballard aside so that he fell. He grabbed Babington by the shoulder and arm, throwing him to the floor beside Ballard. Then one of the pursuivants let go of Poley and knelt upon Ballard's chest, pinning him to the floor.

Satisfied they were all under control, they roped them together and stood them up against the wall to search and examine them. Poley tolerated it with the resignation of one who was no stranger to such procedures, as indeed he wasn't, and who had nothing to fear, as indeed he hadn't, this time. Babington, wide-eyed and shaking, protested in a high querulous voice, demanding to know who they were, what was going on and insisting that the Court should hear of this. No one answered him. Ballard, a tall man with hair and beard as black as Mr Secretary's, was silent and watchful, calculating. No doubt he was fearful, too, and with good reason, but he didn't show it.

Christopher witnessed all this from just inside the door. He had no need to say anything more and neither Babington nor Ballard paid him any attention.

The city official stood before each man in turn and said, 'Who are you? Give me your name.'

Poley answered straightforwardly and, when asked who could vouch for him, said, 'Sir Francis Walsingham, whose messenger I am.'

Babington described himself as Anthony Babington, gentleman of Derbyshire and Lincoln's Inn. Then, recovering himself, he demanded to know who it was who asked. They ignored him.

Ballard drew himself up and gave his name as Captain Fortescue, military gentleman. The city official stared at him. 'Are you known by any other name?'

'People sometimes call me Black Fortescue.'

'What else do they call you?'

'They may call me many things, depending on whether they mean good or ill.' He had a deep voice, controlled and clear.

'Do they ever call you John Ballard, priest?'

'Never to my knowledge. Why should they?'

The official turned to the pursuivants. 'Take him. Let the others go.'

Ballard was bound anew and led out. Christopher said that his expression was set hard like a man determined to resist. Determined he may have been, then, and certainly remained so while held in the Counter prison. But taken later in the Tower he confessed all to the rack, as nearly all do.

That was the end of Christopher's official role in the affair. For what happened next we had only Poley's account, which was true enough but, as usual, showed its author in a fair light and was not quite complete. He said that he and Babington stayed talking a while. Babington was shaken, white as a ghost, fearful that the plot had been discovered. Poley persuaded him that the authorities were very hot on priests entering the country in order to preach sedition and that somehow they must have discovered Ballard's real name and his Fortescue alias, perhaps from spies in the seminary that sent him. If they had suspected the plot they would have arrested Babington, Poley insisted, and probably himself too, but they had shown no interest. It was clear that they were simply after a priest.

Babington, calming, accepted this but worried that Ballard might under torture reveal the plot and the names of all the plotters. He and the others must flee, he said. It would be best to flee abroad but they had no papers so would have to go to ground in the country. Poley urged that they should simply lie low, do nothing to indicate that they feared arrest and meanwhile bring their plot to early fruition. Killing the Queen and restoring the old religion was now their best – perhaps only – route to long-term safety. Or so Poley said he said. Babington agreed, allegedly, and Poley left the house pleading other business, though in fact to report to me and Mr Secretary.

We learned later from Babington's many examinations – I think he was interrogated nine times – that Poley had urged him to flee, saying he would do the same himself. This was no doubt to preserve his reputation among the plotters and with Thomas Morgan and others on the Continent. He could have suggested it to Mr Secretary, who might have agreed so long as we had sufficient notice to apprehend the plotters, but as so often with men like Poley their complications serve but to confound themselves. It was because this cover story was not planned and properly disseminated that we had later to protect Poley's reputation by imprisoning him for a period.

The plotters scattered, two to Cheshire, one to Worcestershire, but the rest never got far from London. They fled north of the city to St John's Wood where they hid for about ten days. Finding country living hard and unforgiving, as any animal could have told them, they finally tottered into the town of Harrow, ragged, filthy, starving scarecrows. Begging for food brought them to notice of the authorities and they took their next meal in the Tower, which must have been a relief, at first.

They did not need racking. In their weakened state they talked readily in exchange for food and rest, Babington no less than the others although he was shown the rack before questioning, to encourage him. This meant I was again distracted from my cipher work since I had to prepare questions and evidence for them to swear. I had personally to confront Babington with the cipher he used in his correspondence with the Queen of Scots. Indeed, I had to help him through it since he was far from expert in these matters. In the presence of a notary public he confirmed that it was the alphabet 'by which only I have written unto the Queen of Scots or received letters from her'. Asked to recall from memory the last letter he had

had from her – not knowing of course that we had added the forged paragraph to it – he stated that she had 'required to know the names of the six gentlemen: that she might give her advice thereupon'. This was very satisfactory, to me especially, since it showed that our forgery was swallowed whole. Although I was relieved when it was not included in the trial of the Queen of Scots – who would rightly have denied it, of course – I suspect it would have stood the test.

I have said that Christopher had no further involvement in the case but he was greatly curious about the Tower and the details of examination and torture, especially the circumstances in which torture licences were granted. He wanted to know how prisoners responded, at which points they talked. He even wanted descriptions of the cellars and chambers in which such examinations were conducted. Most people were rightly fearful of such things and preferred not to hear about them lest they had nightmares. But Christopher wanted to know it. He was like that about everything. He wanted to know everything.

'Is this for your plays?' I asked. 'You want to have someone racked on stage?'

'One day, maybe. Torture is so terrible, it fascinates me as much as it frightens me.'

'Yet you want to witness what frightens you. You enjoy it?'

'I want to confront my demons. Don't you?'

'I have seen enough of racking and torture and do not like it. No demons beckon me to it.'

'You are a simple man, Thomas. Simplicity is a virtue.'

Christopher was very persuasive. When he wanted something his eyes shone with wanting, like a child's. And, like a child, he persisted until his whole being seemed suffused with longing. Eventually, swallowing my aversion, I took him to witness one of the interrogations of Babington. He was not being racked, which was a relief to me, so it was not in a cellar but in a large upper room in the Tower with windows overlooking the river. When we arrived the examining officials and lawyers were still waiting for him to be brought up from the cells. They talked among themselves with some good humour, like men before a market. When brought in in chains he made a pale and pathetic figure, gazing in wonder at so many of importance gathered to hear him. He was eager to speak and several times answered so fully and repetitively that he had to be stopped. Presumably he hoped to ingratiate himself by being helpful.

'He hopes for mercy,' Christopher whispered to me. 'Will he get it?'

'No.' I had heard from Mr Secretary that the Queen had ordered her would-be murderers to be executed in the most prolonged and painful manner the law permitted, that their suffering should be an example to all. 'Unless from God.'

'He hopes in vain then.'

We sat through the full examination, two hours during which Babington confessed enough to have himself hanged, drawn and quartered several times over. That was the purpose of his repeated examinations, to ensure that he gave evidence sufficient to condemn himself and all his colleagues, especially Ballard. In fact, they all condemned themselves readily enough, though Ballard only after significant persuasion. When the time came to take Babington back to the cells he had to be helped to his feet – he had been permitted to sit after the first hour – and I remember still the slow clank of his chains as he shuffled away, a bent and sorry figure. At the door he stopped and turned back to us all, saying in a weak hoarse voice, 'Gentlemen, I am truly sorry to have caused you trouble. We never intended—'

He never finished because the gaolers took hold and yanked him away.

'Another simple man,' whispered Christopher. 'But a foolish one, which – happily – you are not.'

Afterwards I persuaded a sub-warden of the Tower to show us the cells. We first saw those where noble prisoners were held, along with the wealthy whose fate was not decided. They were half-decent quarters such as I have now, thanks to your interest in me, sir. Some were truly generous, such as those in which Sir Walter Ralegh was subsequently imprisoned for sixteen years while writing his great history of the world. Christopher, of course, knew Ralegh and his fellow free-thinkers and it is ironic that we lingered at that door, not knowing how their fates would entwine.

Then we were taken down to the lower cells where the meaner sort were kept, along with those already condemned or awaiting torture. These – as perhaps you have heard, sir, though I hope you have been spared personal acquaintance? – are dark, damp, noisome places often lit only by gratings at ground level and sometimes not at all, unless by flares and candles in the hands of gaolers. We traversed a long tunnel past these grim cellars at the end of which was a great door.

Our warden paused. 'Do you wish to see the chamber, sirs? The confessing chamber, we call it. It is in use today.'

I knew what that meant and would have been content to stop there but Christopher's thirst for the vicarious was not slaked. He wanted to go in.

'I must ask you to be silent for fear of interrupting the conversation,' our warden cautioned us.

The great door creaked back to reveal a flight of wooden stairs leading down into a cavernous basement. The air was heavy with smoke from torches in the walls and the only other light came from two gratings giving onto the moat. The floor was solid rock laid with rushes. In the middle of the chamber, lit by four torches on poles, was the rack. Since that machine seems to have fallen out of use now and there is even, I hear, talk of a law to prohibit it, I shall briefly describe it for you, sir. It comprised a rectangular wooden frame with sides about a foot high and inside at each end a wooden roller which could be turned upon a ratchet by poles inserted into slots. Attached to each of these rollers were two chains to which the hands and feet of the victim were tied. When the victim was stretched between them his whole body was lifted from the ground and suspended under tension, which was increased, notch by notch, according to whether he answered the questions. His shoulders, hips, ankles, knees, elbows and wrists were gradually pulled apart and dislocated, and his tendons and muscles so stretched that those who resisted long were often unable to walk or stand at their trials. It is said there were some few who withstood all torture without confessing, but they were rare. Almost all talked, the sensible ones merely upon being shown the rack, sometimes with their predecessor still stretched upon it.

There was a racking that day. A man in a dark tunic and breeches was suspended, while a man at each roller held the poles in their ratchets. Three other men were at the side of the rack, one kneeling to address the victim. Another, a lawyer, to judge by his robe, stood watching. A third, younger, sat at a low desk with quill, paper and ink. The scene was lit by the flickering flares and the only sounds were the murmured words of the kneeling man, which we could not make out.

Our warden stopped us some yards away. 'We must not intrude,' he whispered, as if it were a religious ceremony.

As in a sense it was. The man being racked was the priest John Ballard. Christopher recognised him and murmured in my ear. I think I have said enough to you, sir, to indicate that I have never been as much at ease with racking and other tortures as some men are. I don't think Mr Secretary or Lord Burghley were, either, though they accepted its necessity and occasionally attended a racking themselves to be sure that the correct questions were put. I accepted the necessity of it but the fact, the sight of it, left me out of sorts for days. I endured it only by reminding myself of the many of my own faith, loyal men and women, who had been stretched, hanged and burned alive during the reign of Bloody Mary. Then it was

Protestants who were racked, now Catholics, almost as if it were a rite of passage. Save that the Catholics were not racked merely for being such but only if they threatened the security of the state. That, at least, was how it was supposed to be.

I could not look at Ballard's suspended body for long but Christopher, whose face I fancied was paler than usual, stared intently. It was as if he sought to absorb, to soak up everything from the scene. The man kneeling by the rack spoke in an undertone, softly, monotonously, as if mouthing a catechism. He paused for some seconds, during which the only sounds were the crackling of the torches and the breeze through the gratings. Then he raised his forefinger and nodded at the man with the pole at the head of the rack. Speaking distinctly this time, he said, 'One more.'

The man removed his pole from one notch and carefully inserted it into the next. Then he leaned against the pole and pushed it forward. There was a single loud click of the ratchet.

For another second or two there was silence, then a small but very distinct plop as something was plucked out of its joint. This was immediately followed by a prolonged strangled sound, not a full-throated scream but one that sounded as if it too were being racked, pulled from the throat of John Ballard. The priest's face showed white through his beard, rigid, staring upwards, his mouth and eyes open wide, his cheeks wet and quivering. When the scream stopped the kneeling man said something to which there must have been an answer because he motioned again to the man at the ratchet, who eased it a notch back to where it had been. The kneeling man moved closer to Ballard's head, putting his ear almost to his mouth. Ballard said something and the man turned towards the scribe at the desk, again with words we could not distinguish, which the scribe took down.

Thus was John Ballard's confession extracted, a word, a name, a sentence at a time. It was later read aloud for him in court, he being too weak to profess it himself. Not that it was needed by then because the confessions of Babington and the others, obtained without racking, were sufficient to have them all hanged, drawn and quartered at St Giles-in-the-Fields – which was where they had met and plotted. The drawing of their guts was done as slowly and carefully as could be, the Queen having said she wanted an example made of these men 'for more terror'. I witnessed that too, again with Christopher. They were done over two days and we were there to see the ending of Ballard, Chidiocke Tycheborne, John Savage and Anthony Babington. There was such a crush of people we could not see all of it clearly and, neither of us being tall, we had to peer over many men's heads.

Ballard died too soon to be drawn alive, his head still in the noose, such was his state following his racking. Unlike those he seduced to his cause he did not suffer being laid out on the ground while the executioner knelt between his legs and cut off his private parts. Then the executioner would throw them into the fire or, if he were minded, into the crowd. Nor did Ballard suffer the evisceration of his bowels and gut as the executioner's knife opened him from crotch to ribs, pulling out his intestines and organs hand over hand and holding them aloft for all to see before throwing them to the flames or feeding them to the dogs. Some said that Babington sighed as his heart was plucked out but we were not close enough to hear.

I tell you this, sir, not because I enjoyed such spectacles – though it was impossible not to watch if you were anywhere near – but so that you understand the significance of my conversation with Christopher afterwards. I believe it had a bearing on his own death seven years later.

We left the execution that day with a sense of relief – for me, at least – and threaded our way towards Christopher's lodging without either of us having expressed any intention of where to go. I think we were both somewhat dazed by what we had witnessed and it was a while before we spoke. For me, the jostling, noisy, smelly streets were a relief for once, the buffets and hazards of daily life a pleasure again. It was not until we were approaching Hog Lane that either of us spoke.

'What are you thinking?' he asked. 'Now, this minute?'

'I was thinking of those men, the rackers and executioners, whose daily task that is. Whether it makes them morbid or whether their senses are so blunted that they become like cider-presses, heedless of the apples they crush.'

'But you accept it has to be done so that God's will be fulfilled?'

'Yes. Though I prefer that others should do it.'

'You count yourself a good Christian, Thomas. Is what we've seen Christian? What about mercy?'

'It is our Christian duty to defend God's purpose and God's word. Mercy is God's prerogative.'

'Which is exactly what Father Ballard would say if it were you or me on the rack.'

I was well aware of this uncomfortable truth and tried not to think about it because I saw no way around it. 'If it is God's will that such things should happen, whoever does them, in order that we may come to His truth and be reconciled to Him, then we have to accept it. His ways may be mysteries to us now but when we are brought before Him all will be revealed and all shall be reconciled.'

'Thus a multitude of individual sufferings is the price of reconciliation with the Almighty. A price worth paying. Is that what you truly believe?'

'I say God works in mysterious ways, ways beyond our comprehension.'

'But if someone says the price is too high, that they reject reconciliation on such terms, they spurn God, what would happen to them?'

'They would be punished everlastingly.'

'By the ever-merciful?' There was a playful light in his eyes. 'So we suffer in this world or in the next. We are doomed to suffer either way. But what if there is no next world? Supposing that beyond us, after us, beyond the sky, there is nothing? No thing. Yet if there is after all another world, then we suffer in both. Is that your idea of a just and merciful God?'

There are men who relish such arguments, delighting in

wordy twists and turns, but I am not one of them. Arguments like that always lead so quickly to extreme conclusions that within a few sentences I find myself forced into positions I would never have chosen. Words are slippery, easily disguised, their meanings changing with context. You and I, sir, may use the same words but mean them differently, making us honest neither with each other nor with ourselves. Do you not think?

Very well, I go on.

I stopped Christopher in the street when he spoke as he did then. 'You cannot, must not say such things. They would make you a free-thinker, an atheist.'

He raised his arms. 'Atheist, theist, deist – I care nothing for any ists. I care for the mind and I follow thought as far and as honestly as I can. I have no time for stories invented to persuade us we never really die.' Then he smiled and patted my arm. 'I'm sorry, Thomas, I don't mean to trouble you and make you unhappy.'

'I'm not unhappy. But I worry for your sake.' That was only half true. Such thoughts, rarely expressed and as dangerous then as now, unsettled me. They watered seeds of doubt planted deep in my soul. Some men have the gift of faith, believing with a serenity that is proof against doubt. Mr Secretary was one. I am not.

I hope this does not shock you, sir, and I hope His Majesty will not think worse of me if you report it. I confess freely now because at my age I am close enough to the answers to these questions not to worry what men think of me. Either

I shall find that religion is true and that Christopher and all doubters were wrong, or I shall know nothing. I shall be as I was before I was born and never know that the doubters were right. There is nothing to fear from that. But I tell you this so that you understand that he thought these thoughts himself from early days, long before the stories of free-thinking that surrounded him at his death. I ask again, could that be the reason for His Majesty's interest in him?

If so, His Majesty will wish to know that both before and after his death Christopher was accused of scoffing at religion and of being part of Sir Walter Ralegh's School of Night. That was a supposed cabal of free-thinkers, though I don't believe Ralegh ever organised anything as formal. Whether Christopher was part of it, I do not know. Robert Greene, a player and writer not known for his kindly opinions of others, wrote in his death-bed repentance of what he called Christopher's diabolical atheism, saying, 'he hath said ... like the fool in his heart: There is no God.' Also another play-maker, Thomas Kyd, who had sometime shared rooms with Christopher and who was later arrested for the Dutch Church libel which I investigated, claimed that Christopher had 'monstrous opinions'. He said that he scoffed and jested at scripture, called St Paul a juggler and accused Christ of unnatural love for St John. Among papers found in Kyd's room were some that questioned the truths of divine scripture. He said they were Christopher's and must have been mixed with his when they shared a room. But he was being racked when he said these things, pleading for his life. He was being racked for the Dutch Church libel, of which he was innocent, poor man. He was released after racking, I am glad to say.

Maybe Christopher did speak in that way with his friends. He never did with me. Whether it was from gentleness, sensing that my faith was fragile, or whether he thought I might report him, I know not. He would tease, certainly, but I never knew him mocking or cruel as others said he could be. Yet he did more to bring me to my current state than any amount of mockery, jibing or abuse could have done. He never sought to persuade me, he only ever questioned. And his questions remain.

Where did he get these ideas? The Ancients, perhaps, maybe even the Book of Job, but mostly I suspect from within himself. He was well versed in scripture, better than many clergy. He studied deeply, but other men have studied without being led to doubt. May God forgive him, wherever he be now, though I truly believe that what led him into doubt was honesty, honesty of the mind. Not malice or vanity or ignorance or passion. He said to me once that we have a duty to Reason because we have a duty to be honest.

We were near his lodging when we had the exchange I have just related. 'Come in,' he said. 'It is warm enough to sit in the garden and talk of lighter things. If Widow Turner favours you she may bring us cider.' He smiled. 'That may be a sign.'

We did drink cider in the garden that morning and Mary Turner was most welcoming. She sent a girl to attend to us and then joined us for a while, albeit mostly addressing Christopher. However, when she stood to leave us, saying we must have theatre business to discuss, she smiled at me. This encouraged me to linger briefly after Christopher left for the playhouse. She asked me about the theatre, assuming I was as much involved as her two lodgers, and it turned out she had never seen a play, fearing they were rough and unruly events. I offered to escort her one day but had then to confess that I was not a player or poet or play-maker myself. I told her I did write but in a private capacity for Sir Francis Walsingham and other gentlemen of the Court. I hoped that would impress her and returned to Whitehall with pleasing anticipation. It did something to distract me from the executions.

CHAPTER SEVEN

At about this time Thomas Walsingham, Mr Secretary's cousin, increasingly featured in our work. A trusted man who had done well in Paris, he now moved into Mr Secretary's house in Seething Lane to be of more intimate assistance, especially when Mr Secretary was struck down by the stone. This was happening ever more frequently. There were periods when Sir Francis kept to his room for weeks at a time in pain and sickness, unable to attend Court. His secretary Francis Mylles kept him informed and he continued to give general directions but could not attend to the detail he loved.

Thomas, like Mr Secretary himself, was a generous patron of poetry and the arts and I cannot now say whether it was through that that he and Christopher came to know each other well or whether through working for us. Most likely the former, since Christopher did little for us after the Babington business apart from occasional courier work, though I suspect he saw more of Poley, Skeres and Frizer than I knew. At some point Thomas took Frizer into his household at Scadbury Park in Chislehurst, Kent. It was not far from

London and must have meant that Christopher and Frizer saw more of each other. Whatever their differences, they then shared an interest in pleasing their mutual patron. It was to prove a fateful alliance.

My own work was almost all-consuming. It was the time of our war with Spain and of the great Armada sent to invade us which, thanks to weather, Sir Francis Drake and God's grace, was prevented. Little known then, and not at all now, we had other means of prevention at work. We intercepted their letters, deciphered their codes, divined their intentions and sabotaged many of their fleet's water and powder barrels before it had even embarked. I would spend whole nights deciphering and still work through the day after.

I said 'almost' all-consuming. In the few intervals between sleep and work I courted Mary Turner, visiting her house whenever I could with gifts and favours. She proved amenable. We walked gently together, our minds hand-in-hand as it were, to our eventual marriage, for which great blessing I am ever grateful. My visits to her meant that I saw a little of Christopher there, though not on our business. He was becoming a great figure by then, no longer the humble student – not that he was ever really humble, merely unknown – I had first met. His plays had great success and his poems were sought after in the bookshop by St Paul's where writers and printers gathered. I never saw any of his plays while he lived. That was my lack and is still my regret. I have seen one or two since and found in them much to question him about.

There was no hiding my courtship from him, of course. He

teased me about it. He would greet me with a smile and say, 'Ah, Thomas, what brings you here? Is it the air, the prospect, are there letters to copy? Or are you in search of rhymes to please our landlady? In which case, Watson and I will furnish you with plenty to further your cause.' And to Mary he would say in my presence, 'Goodwife Turner, I must warn you against this fellow, he is a ruffian and a great deceiver, a thief of women's hearts. I must lend you my sword.'

But then he would leave us to ourselves. I discovered later that he spoke kindly of me to Mary, saying I was an honest thief who, having once stolen a heart, would keep it safe and be true to it. It was that sword of his, though, that led me into further official dealings with him.

I did not witness the affray. It was really nothing to do with Christopher except by mischance. It happened one fine September morning when I was at Mary's house with apples for her that Mr Secretary had had delivered from Barn Elms to be distributed among us who worked for him. I had been up all night finishing a great hunk of work and had awarded myself a morning of rest before embarking on the next. Both the poet Watson and Christopher were there and the four of us shared a cheerful breakfast, the two of them causing much merriment with demonstrations of smoking tobacco in pipes, a habit then coming into fashion. It seemed difficult to get these engines going and when they did there was so much smoke that the engineers spent more time coughing and spluttering than enjoying it. Mary said that her washing, which was drying by the fire, smelled for days afterwards of tobacco smoke. Later, when he was being racked, Thomas Kyd claimed that Christopher would say that all who did not enjoy tobacco and boys were fools. Perhaps he did but from the few times I saw him with pipe and tobacco I would not say he enjoyed it; he had to work too hard at it for pleasure. As for boys, I never knew him for a sodomite, nor did he ever mention it in my hearing, though in his play *King Edward II* he had the king buggered with a red-hot poker. Do you know that play, sir? Well, I doubt the King would like it. Kings do not like to see the deaths of kings, especially deaths such as that. But, as I have said, Christopher was ever gentle with me and there might have been many things he did not mention. Certainly, he was not always so gentle with others.

He left the house first that morning to see his collaborator, the other play-maker I had briefly met. As he went he buckled on a sword he had bought, although so far as I know he had not then achieved the status of gentleman that entitled him to bear one in public. No matter, perhaps, because companies of players often had swords for their stage fights. Watson left the house shortly after – he always wore a sword when in the streets, being entitled to it – and Mary and I were left to converse in peace, that free intercourse by which we establish the compatibility of minds which is the bedrock of good marriage. We were interrupted by a great hammering on the door. Mary bade both servants answer before showing herself.

It was two neighbours, both women. Bidden enter, they breathlessly described a great fight at the end of the street in Hog Lane involving Mary's lodgers and a man who was killed. So confused were their accounts, delivered simultaneously, that it sounded at first as if the fight had been between Watson and Christopher and that one of them was dead. Then, when we had calmed them enough, we learned that although one was wounded – they were confused as to which – he did not look like to die. But another man whom no one knew was dead.

We hurried down to Hog Lane and there found a crowd gathered over the body of a young man by the ditch. He was on his back with a sword wound to his chest an inch or more wide. There was not much blood but he was without doubt dead. His eyes were wide, staring skywards as if in surprise. Beside him stood Tom Watson, his sword sheathed. He was stooping and holding a rag to a bleeding wound in his thigh. Christopher stood a few feet off, his sword also sheathed. Of all there he alone looked calm and untroubled. He held up his hand when he saw us. 'It's all right. No need for worry. Thomas's wound is slight.' He nodded at the body. 'And the dog is dead.'

Someone had summoned the parish constable, a tailor called Wylde. He was not a robust fellow and approached the two men fearfully, as if they might go for him. But Watson reassured him, saying, 'We will make statements, we have nothing to hide. I killed the man in self-defence as my friend Mr Marlowe can vouch. So too can some here who witnessed it.' The constable bade them accompany him to the justice, Sir Owen Hopton, Lieutenant of the Tower. As they went

Christopher turned to me and said in an undertone, 'It is true, we are both innocent. But can you help if need be?'

It took time for the full story to emerge. I give it here in short form because it was later put about that Christopher had killed the man in a brawl. He was not brawling and he killed no one. It was the dead man, William Bradley, son of a Holborn innkeeper, who was the brawler, and known for one. He had a grievance against Tom Watson over a debt that he, Bradley, owed the brother of Edward Alleyn, the leading actor of those days who took the great parts in Christopher's plays. Alleyn's brother had hired Watson's brother-in-law, an attorney, to take Bradley to court. Bradley had threatened the attorney with violence, upon which the attorney, Alleyn's brother and Watson himself had threatened him. Blaming Watson for this, Bradley waited for him in Hog Lane that day, presumably to give him a beating.

Instead it was Christopher who came first from Mary's house and turned the corner into Hog Lane where he was accosted by Bradley, who knew him for an intimate of Watson's. They had words and Christopher – never one to back down from a fight – gave as good as he got. Swords were drawn and they were having at each other, though with no blood yet drawn, when Watson appeared. Bradley saw him and cried, 'Art thou now come? Then I will have a bout with thee.' He turned upon Watson and Christopher stood aside. There was no doubt, Christopher said, that Bradley by then meant to kill. He wielded his sword in his right hand and his dagger in his left, the latter for parrying close thrusts, and the fury of his assault drove Watson back to the edge of the ditch where he had no choice but to stand his ground and fight. He parried one of Bradley's thrusts and counter-attacked, straightening his arm quickly enough to evade Bradley's knife-parry. Bradley's momentum carried him forward onto Watson's blade, which sank six inches into his chest. He stumbled, coughed and cried out as Watson withdrew his blade. Then he dropped his weapons, sank to his knees, made a noise between a sigh and a gurgle, and rolled onto his back where he lay, one leg hooked beneath the other, staring heavenwards.

What struck Christopher was how it was over on an instant. One moment there was a man, a life, a voice, a vivid moving presence, a whole world in that man's head. Another moment and there was merely a carcass, food for rats and worms, that whole world, everything that man knew and would have said or done, gone in an instant. And immediately everything else, the rest of the teeming world, was as if he had never been. 'Nothing happens when you die,' I remember him saying. 'It is not even an event, just a ceasing. Why fear it?'

'We fear God's judgement and punishment for our sins.' I said such things with confidence then.

'We fear nothingness more. Extinction, total, eternal, everlasting. That is what we really fear. We would prefer Hell.'

'Easily said when you're not in it.'

'Hell keeps hope alive, Thomas. There's always the possibility of the alternative. But think on nothingness, think hard on nothing. See how long you can bear it.'

That was typical of him, of how he spoke and thought.

The law took its usual leisurely course. They were sent to Newgate gaol on suspicion of murder and the inquest next day decided that Thomas Watson slew William Bradley in self-defence, not by felony, and that Christopher had no part in it. But they could not be released without the Queen's official pardon, which would take months, and so they were returned to Newgate. I had by then reported to Mr Secretary, who always wanted to know the doings of our agents or anyone associated with us. He told me to arrange bail for Christopher. I engaged a lawyer from Clifford's Inn whom we often called upon and a prosperous tradesman we knew, a horner from Smithfield. In return for favours past and to come they stood bail for twenty pounds apiece. Christopher was freed and bound over to appear at the next Newgate sessions in a couple of months, but Watson had to remain in that stinking hole.

This took precious days during which the flood of work nearly overwhelmed me. Mr Secretary demanded the same quick results with no allowance made for other tasks he imposed, and when I protested, mildly enough, he replied that those privileged to perform the Lord's work should not complain of the yoke. In fairness, he was as exacting of himself as of others, but that did not make for an easy life.

I collected Christopher from Newgate. He was heartily glad to be freed but worried for Watson since many there died of fever, it being such an ill-favoured place with airs to make you retch and a stench that lingered about you for days after. He and Watson were thrown into the common cell for their first night, an evil dark place called Stone Hold. It was underground and overcrowded, with some prisoners chained to the dripping walls. There was one candle set in the middle but the rats took it and thereafter ran freely across men's legs in the dark, nibbling their clothes. One poor shivering wretch had no clothes at all, having been there, he said, nine years.

But Christopher and Watson had access to money and next morning, after words with their gaoler, they were moved to their own upper-floor cell with a window. They had doubtless been thrown into Stone Hold in order to encourage a better bribe. My experience here in King's Bench gaol persuades me it is the same in all gaols. Conditions here improved greatly as soon as it was known that you, sir, were taking an interest in me on behalf of the Court. I am treated almost as a guest, for which I thank you heartily. I am most anxious to be of use to His Majesty but still I do not understand what of Christopher Marlowe he wants to hear from me. It would help my memory and my interpretation if you could afford me some hint of the direction of the King's interest.

Very well, I shall continue with everything. Tom Watson was duly pardoned at the next sessions, at the same time as Christopher's bail was discharged. They appeared before Sir Roger Manwood, the Kent judge who had been patron for Christopher's scholarship. He despatched the matter swiftly. I suspect Mr Secretary, also a Kent man, might have spoken to him, since when he asked me the date of the session he asked also that I should find out who was due to sit. Although

Christopher was discharged immediately and Watson's pardon recommended, it was some months more before his pardon came and he was released. He died, poor man, not many years later of a sickness of the chest caught in Newgate. So William Bradley had his revenge from beyond the grave.

Watson was acknowledged a great poet, especially of the Latin, though I do not know that he is much read now. He asked Christopher to see his last work published with a dedication to his patroness, the Lady Sidney, whom you will recall was Mr Secretary's beloved only daughter and widow to the great Sir Philip Sidney. All this Christopher performed dutifully.

It was not the only epitaph he composed. He wrote most generously in Latin of his patron, Sir Roger, who may of course have helped him in sundry other ways of which I knew nothing. I never knew Christopher to be short of money – at least, he never complained of it – and I suspect he received generous patronage in his youth. Later, of course, his plays and verses made him famous and he must have earned well though he was always careful with money, perhaps even tight. But when we were paying him he never asked for more, as many did. In fact, Mr Secretary always paid well: 'Knowledge is never too dear,' he would say, as I may have told you already. He knew very well how costly our business can be because he often had to pay for it himself. Queen Elizabeth always preferred her subjects to spend on her behalf.

You ask about fights. I have already mentioned his

readiness and the Bradley business was not his only affray in those years. He was brought before Sir Owen Hopton a second time for threatening the constables in Holywell Street and was bound over to keep the peace on promise of payment of twenty pounds, to be raised if necessary from the sale of any goods and property he might acquire. Then in Canterbury he fought a duel with one William Corkine, a musician of the cathedral. I do not know what about but neither was injured. Corkine started legal proceedings afterwards but dropped them. Around the time of Christopher's death Thomas Kyd and Richard Baines wrote that he was wont to cause 'sudden privy injuries to men'. It was true he would not hold back in argument and he was certainly prepared to settle matters with his fists, as I have said, but I never knew him start the argument.

You ask whether his arguments were personal, whether he had personal relations with those he fought, whether the fights were about those relations. I cannot help. I never heard that they were, or were not. You see, there were long periods when we saw nothing of each other, our daily lives being so different. But I do recall taxing him once over his temper. We were in Mary's house, seated at table. Mary was there but not Watson, so it may have been just after Christopher was released from Newgate. He was telling us how he had learned about counterfeiting coins from another prisoner, John Poole, incarcerated for that crime. He laughed that Newgate had given him 'as good a right to coin as the Queen of England' and that if he found a cunning stamp-maker he would coin French crowns and English shillings. I took him more seriously than perhaps he meant – at the time, anyway – and reminded him that this was a capital offence that could have him boiled in oil. Even jesting about it was dangerous.

'My apologies, your Honour. It is so good to be free that cheerfulness will keep breaking through.'

Mary laughed at that, which provoked me. I warned him against further street fights, saying, 'Your temper leads you by the nose and you are like to get it broken.'

'What you call my temper I call a passion for justice which is as like to lead me to the noose in these times as to a broken nose. Not a danger that threatens you, eh, Thomas?' With that he smiled and nudged me with his foot under the table. Mary smiled too. She was always willing to indulge him.

Indeed yes, sir, indeed he did coin. After a fashion but in a manner close enough to the crime itself as to make no difference, you might say. Of course, it is not my place to ask, sir, but is His Majesty especially interested in coining? Are there perhaps threats to the coin of the realm now and does he wish to hear of this as an example of how—?

Very well, sir, the episode was a couple of years after Mr Secretary died and not long before Christopher's own end. Mr Secretary's death was a terrible thing in our world. In the confusion that followed most of his records were destroyed by Francis Mylles and his household staff. I rushed to Seething Lane to preserve them, since intelligencers who do not know what they have in their records are destined endlessly to repeat themselves in ignorance and failure. But

I was too late. He died in the night and news did not reach me until late the following morning, by which time many papers had been destroyed and some removed by Sir Robert Cecil, Lord Burghley's son, whom Mr Secretary was bringing on in his own image. Some were also removed by Thomas Walsingham. Among those destroyed were many pertaining to my own work. Fortunately, however, I had enough in Whitehall to help me continue deciphering for whomsoever would employ me after.

I stayed for the funeral the following night. It was in darkness in St Paul's churchyard, conducted almost in secrecy as Sir Francis directed, with few mourners, just his immediate family and personal staff. His daughter wept but his wife, who had witnessed more of his suffering, was dry-eyed. I was honoured to be asked to be a pall-bearer along with Francis Mylles and a couple of others. Normally pall-bearers would have been men of Sir Francis's rank but he was buried hurriedly without their knowledge. He was heavy, it was raining and after the briefest of services we slipped and stumbled several times on the wet grass and mounds as we were led to a corner of the graveyard by the minister bearing a torch. When we eventually found the grave it was too narrow for the coffin to slide in easily and Francis and I had to force it down with our feet, which seemed disrespectful. At one moment Francis got his end down farther than mine so that Mr Secretary was being tipped feet-first into his grave. In pushing my end harder I slipped on the mud at the side and almost tumbled in after him. The grave-diggers were in such haste to finish and get away they might well have buried me with him.

He wished, he had said, for his wife and daughter not to be put to the expense of an elaborate funeral – such as when he had paid for seven hundred mourners at the funeral of his son-in-law, Sir Phillip Sidney – and I suspect the humility and obscurity of a plain funeral seemed to him a more fitting approach to his Maker than pomp and grandeur. That he was confident of meeting his Maker I do not doubt. I wish I had the confidence now to believe as he did. It is thanks to Christopher that I do not.

His last days were consumed by great suffering which he bore with patience and stoicism, seeing it as a cleansing fire he had to pass through before reconciliation with our Lord. It was his old enemy, the stone, that caused such pain. Poley put it about afterwards that his urine came out of his mouth and that there was such stench in his room that none could bear it. It is true that in carrying the coffin, our noses pressed against the sides, we all found a foul smell. But Poley also said that he died of a pox of his yard caught from a whore in Paris, which I cannot believe. Anyway, Poley was not there and, as always with that man, you had to sieve his assertions through a fine net of evidence. He too must be long dead now – I have not heard of him for twenty or more years – but I don't doubt he will be spinning such a yarn in Hell that the Devil himself cannot tell truth from lie.

The passing of Mr Secretary wrought a change in my own life, not for the better. He had been my guide, my mentor, my example, in some ways more a father to me than my own. We were never personal with each other, never intimate, he being naturally a distant man, but there was an understanding between us, a sympathy of mind and purpose, unspoken but known and felt. He was a man of inflexible integrity, there was nothing about him I did not admire, nothing I did not seek to emulate, though I knew I could never match him. As the clods of earth thumped onto his coffin in the dark, and we all stood in silence save for his daughter's weeping, I feared for the future. I suspect we all did.

Chapter Eight

Christopher's coining, sir, of course. I shall tell you, I shall. Please bear with me, I beg you. All these things have a context and it is their contexts that lend significance, give meaning. There is no straight path and I must go roundabout about to bring you home.

There was none who could take Mr Secretary's place, none with his omniscient command of secret matters or his capacity in other areas, such as the building of Dover harbour and promoting of the arts. He was never not at work. The Lord Burghley was more concerned with home matters and the control of money, the Earl of Essex was for overseas adventures and Robert Cecil was not then grown into full estate. In time, as you and the King know well, he would succeed his father most admirably while continuing Mr Secretary's good work.

We servants to Mr Secretary thus found ourselves adrift, searching for new masters among the great men competing with each other for power and influence. Some were taken by Lord Burghley to help him understand where money was spent on secret work and then reduce it severely, some by Robert Cecil who had already grasped the necessity of the security of the state, others by the Earl of Essex who promised much and was loved by the Queen but who in the end sought his own glory more than hers or England's, and paid for it with his head.

I was an Essex man at first, to my regret and cost. All I wanted was to continue to do the state some service and be rewarded but it was hard to know in those confused times what or who – apart from Her Majesty – constituted the state. My hunch and hope was that it was Burghley and the young Cecil, but the Lord Burghley was distant with me. He would not receive me and seemed not to want to know anything I could tell him of Mr Secretary's business. I believe he associated me with spendthrift ways and indeed my subsequent history – Burghley's pursuit of me and my incarceration for debts to the Crown – bears this out. I cannot deny that I mishandled the customs dues my father and then I collected on Her Majesty's behalf, not paying when I should and then finding that the money I had invested – and had intended to pay – was no longer there, or could not be realised. But I assure you, sir, I was never free with matters touching the security of the state, nor with any money associated with it. I could not get access to the Lord Burghley to explain and at that stage was not well known to Robert Cecil.

Thus when I was summoned by the Earl of Essex a few days after the funeral I hurried with high hopes to his house by the Strand. I do not know whether there are such grand men at Court now but Essex was a great figure with a fine red beard, a strong voice, commanding presence and winning ways. It was easy to see why he was a favourite with the Queen. In battle he had shown no fear, it was said. In time he would be shown to have as little judgement but the day he summoned me he was in his pomp.

His Strand house was a great high building and he received me in a large upper room facing the river. It was like a royal court; he reclined in a very large chair on a raised dais, surrounded by friends and admirers. But it was an informal court with a long table laden with sweetmeats and wines to which people helped themselves while walking about and talking. There were ladies there, too, fine ladies dallying with fine gentlemen. It was quite unlike the Queen's Court where all had to stand as she did and there was no dalliance before her, only business. Of which there was much. On seeing me the Earl called out, 'Ah, our spy. Our spy is come, we are for serious matters now.' That made everyone look round and several gathered close to hear what was said.

I was very uncomfortable. He talked about agents in France he wanted me to use to recruit further agents, including one he named in the French Court who was thought to be susceptible. Mr Secretary would never, ever have discussed such matters in public hearing. I expressed willingness to do it because Mary was with child and I had to put bread on our table but I volunteered no opinions or knowledge of my own. Then he said, 'And tell me, what ciphers are you working on now? Which have we broken?'

I couldn't answer. I was stupefied, dumbfounded that such secret matters should be mentioned so casually. Fortunately, he mistook the reason for my silence. 'Forgetful, eh? A spy with no memory?' He laughed, provoking others to laugh with him. 'Perhaps that's as well. The less you remember, the less you can tell the poisonous dwarf, little Robert Cecil, if he tries to lure you away. You wouldn't tell him anything, would you, eh? Is it true you do not know the man and are out of favour with his father?'

'We have barely ever spoken, sir, and his father no longer speaks to me.' It was well known that Essex and Robert Cecil had become rivals at Court, despite having been some years together as children. Or perhaps because of that. Essex was a tall vigorous man whereas Cecil was not only small but hunchbacked. Perhaps childhood rivalries had matured and hardened.

'Good. We do not want any Cecilian plotting here, eh?' They all laughed again at that.

I left, unhappy in many ways but satisfied in one. Hungry, too, but I was not yet in such great favour that I could help myself to sweetmeats from the table.

Christopher, meanwhile, was already employed by Robert Cecil in the manner he had been by Mr Secretary, as an occasional courier of secret papers. This came about through Thomas Walsingham, whose friend he had become. It meant that he saw more of Robert Poley than was healthy for any man, on at least one occasion accompanying him to Scotland with messages from Cecil. As you probably know, sir – the

King certainly does – Robert Cecil was even then quietly cultivating relations with the Scottish Court, preparing for the day when the Queen died.

The coining business was in 1592 when Christopher couriered papers to the Netherlands. Such trips suited him, especially when the theatres were closed because of plague. On this journey he lodged in the port of Flushing – an English port, of course – with Gifford Gilbert, a goldsmith, and Richard Baines, his subsequent traducer. We never had anything to do with the man Gifford Gilbert but he gave us a deal of trouble because in our records he was often confused with Gilbert Gifford, which whom we had much to do, as I have described. The three men must have been getting on reasonably well in order to lodge together but obviously not that well because Baines wrote to the governor of Flushing accusing his two room-mates of counterfeiting. Christopher and Gilbert were arrested and admitted under interrogation to having uttered a counterfeit Dutch shilling, a foreign coin and therefore not an offence. They protested they had intended only to experiment, using Gilbert's skills to see how it was done. In his report, however, the governor said that Christopher and Baines had each accused the other of inducing Gilbert to do it and that they intended to make a business of it. There were many impoverished English Catholics on the Continent then, all desperate for coinage of any sort. Christopher accused Baines of planning to return to his old faith and defect to Rome if the counterfeiting proved successful. The governor reported all this to Lord Burghley and sent the prisoners back to England under close arrest for examination and trial. Baines was not arrested but was compelled to accompany them as a witness.

I give you this detail, sir, to bear in mind when considering the note penned by Baines at the time of Christopher's death. He claimed that Christopher persuaded men to atheism, urged them not to fear bugbears and hobgoblins, and said that the purpose of religion was only to keep men in awe. According to Baines he also said that holy communion would be better administered in a tobacco pipe and that St John the Evangelist was bedfellow to Christ who was a sodomite. I think I have mentioned this already, sir?

Indeed, yes, there may be truth in it. Although Christopher never spoke in this manner in my hearing I could believe it of him when he was in his cups with players and writers. He relished wine, always did, ever more as he grew older. But I don't believe he seriously persuaded men to atheism or heresy. I think it was play for him, play of the mind. He enjoyed argument and provocation. The more dangerous it was, the more he enjoyed it.

It is true, though, that he undermined my faith, as I have said before. Not by such a catalogue of calumnies and heresies as Baines wrote but more subtly and effectively. He forced me to think.

However, his coining misfortune – if that's what it was – brought good fortune to me. I was at home with Mary trying to match the rents from our properties with the debts incurred in buying them when a liveried messenger from

Robert Cecil summoned me to Whitehall. He received me in the old map room where I had previously worked. Although he was smaller than me and a hump-back – so much that the Queen would call him her imp or dwarf or monkey – whenever I was with him he somehow made me feel it was I who was the smaller. He was courteous enough but his intensity and incisiveness were daunting. When I was introduced on that occasion he stared at me in silence as if trying to make up his mind about me from my appearance. Then he dismissed his secretary and we were alone.

'My father knows you and has told me of your work for Sir Francis.'

'I had that honour, sir.'

'You are familiar with Christopher Marlowe, the poet?'

'I am, sir, but have not seen him these many months.'

'And you have worked for the Earl of Essex.'

That was a statement rather than a question. 'I went to France on his behalf, sir, but it did not turn out well.' Indeed it did not; the Earl's instructions were confused and his demands impossible and I fell from favour. But I will not go into that now.

There was another silence. He stared at me with the detachment born of absolute confidence in one's own position in the world. 'Do you still consider yourself servant to the Earl of Essex?'

'No, sir. Nor did I ever. He employed me very occasionally. Though I also did some small cipher work for him.'

He nodded. 'I have a task for you if you wish it. But it may earn you the Earl's active disfavour since it will associate you with me and my father.'

'I should be grateful, sir.' Association with Robert Cecil, and through him with his father, was my only hope of regaining state service.

He sat at the desk his father and Mr Secretary used when I worked in that room. My own small desk and chair were still in the corner. He indicated to me to draw up the chair. Then he told me what had happened in Flushing, adding that Christopher and Gifford Gilbert were to be examined in public by his father, the Lord Treasurer, and that if he found there was a case against them they would be sent for trial. In which case it was likely they would be found guilty and hang. 'I have no opinion of the man Gilbert,' he concluded, 'but I do not want Marlowe hanged.'

He wanted me to attend the hearing with Christopher and to confer with him beforehand, ensuring that he spoke soberly and respectfully, voicing no outrageous opinions. 'You dealt with him for Sir Francis with evident success. But he is known for outbursts of intemperate speech and behaviour. You must urge moderation and ensure that he pleads only the account he has already given to the governor of Flushing – that they never intended serious coining, that it was done only as playful experiment while awaiting ship for home and was anyway not with English currency. My father is aware of the work he did for Sir Francis and of his occasional use to me in conveying messages to the Scottish Court, but these must on no account be mentioned in public.

You must also ensure that Marlowe makes no mention of his play-making. My father knows of it, of course, but has not the fondness for playhouses that Sir Francis had. He would not react well to a plea of extenuating circumstances arising from poetry. If called upon to give evidence on Marlowe's behalf, as you may be, you must confine yourself to swearing him a God-fearing subject of the Queen, loyal to her church and to God. Nothing else. Do you think you can do that?'

I gave him the assurance he wanted.

'Thomas Walsingham will also be available to give evidence. Between you, you must make it easy for my father to find both men loyal and sober subjects who regret their ill-considered youthful prank and intend no more of it. You are sure you can do that?'

'Yes, sir.' His tone and manner suggested I might have found some difficulty with it but I was steeped in professional deceit far enough to have no problem with minor perjury. Anyway, I truly believed – and believe – that Christopher was loyal to the Queen and England, if not to his God.

'If this goes well there may be other work following,' Robert Cecil concluded. 'Unless of course you choose to continue your involvement with the Earl of Essex.'

Thus I came over the next several years to perform various tasks for Sir Robert, as he became. It was mostly deciphering and was never continuous employment as under Mr Secretary, but it kept the wolf from the door when I was imprisoned for my debts and Mary had to manage our properties and our customs dues. He always treated me well and was considerate of Mary in our distress. But my work for him earned me the enmity of the Earl of Essex and his followers, with consequences that long outlived Sir Robert. They pursue me still. Hence you see me here, sir. There were consequences for Christopher, too, but of more mortal nature.

CHAPTER NINE

Lord Burghley conducted the examination of Christopher and Gifford Gilbert in his chambers in Whitehall Palace. They were large enough for Privy Council meetings to be held there when not with the Queen and he had his own mahogany desk from Italy, inlaid and magnificent. There was also a long oak table with carved high-backed chairs. The windows gave onto the river and its traffic.

Our meeting was twice postponed because the Queen was at Hampton Court or Windsor and Lord Burghley with her. There was rarely a day when he did not see her and, despite their occasional troubles – as when he and Mr Secretary were banned from Court after the execution of the Queen of Scots – there was trust and even fondness between them. He had served her when she was a vulnerable young princess in danger of the executioner's block herself and she had learned to trust him then. Later, when he lay dying, she visited his death-bed. I never heard that she did that for any other commoner.

Lord Burghley was as formidable and forbidding as Mr

Secretary, though short and broad where Mr Secretary was tall and angular. He had a calm, comfortable face and a fine well-trimmed beard. His voice was quiet but he spoke very directly with no words wasted. His gaze, like his son's, was unsettling. It was not hostile or challenging but it was assessing and impersonal, as if you were a piece of furniture he might choose either to buy, or simply to pass by. You felt under judgement and that judgement, for good or ill, would be final.

When I entered his chamber that morning there was him Thomas Walsingham, Ingram Frizer and William Davison, Lord Burghley's secretary. Lord Burghley acknowledged my bow with a nod while talking to Thomas, who smiled a greeting. Frizer stood on the fringe of the group. I was surprised to see him although I knew by then that Thomas had taken him into his household. We nodded, each probably as surprised as the other. William Davison, busy with pens and papers from a previous meeting, gave a brief conspiratorial glance. He and I were on friendly terms, sharing a common understanding of what it was to serve great men, in his case women – or a woman – too. He had been the Queen's junior secretary when she signed the warrant for the execution of the Queen of Scots, some five years before. He had quite properly delivered the warrant forthwith to the Privy Council who had immediately sent it to Fotheringay, where Queen Mary was held and where the deed was promptly done. Her little dog, I heard, licked the blood that spouted from her neck when her head rolled onto the floor.

Queen Elizabeth was furious when she learned that her

cousin was so promptly executed. She blamed anyone but herself and banned his Lordship and Mr Secretary from Court. Poor unfortunate William Davison was punished for his promptitude by immediate imprisonment, the Queen demanding he be hanged. He was spared by the silent intercession of Lord Burghley and Mr Secretary, who sent me to Newgate with letters for his release. I then delivered him to Barn Elms where he remained until Lord Burghley and Mr Secretary resumed their positions at Court, after which Lord Burghley made him one of his servants, taking care that he never appeared within sight of the Queen again. Her Majesty chose not to enquire whether he had been hanged.

I stood at a respectful distance from the group but after a while Lord Burghley beckoned me closer. 'Mr Phelippes, you like Sir Thomas here are acquainted with one of the prisoners, I understand?'

'With Mr Marlowe, please, your Lordship.'

'He associates with players. You follow the players?'

'Little, your Lordship, but I know of his work. He has loyally helped us with our own work—'

'I know what he has done for the Queen. But he sails close to the wind in the playhouses. Do you think he sees one as giving him licence for the other?'

The thought had not occurred to me. 'I have never heard him express such—'

'Do you believe him guilty or innocent in the matter before us?'

'Neither, my Lord.' It was an unconsidered response

but happily apt, as it turned out. Lord Burghley's eyes levelled upon mine, awaiting elaboration. 'I do not believe he intended to be a coiner but can believe he might have thought counterfeiting foreign coin a harmless game to play at.'

'And you consider him loyal? You do not suspect him of planning to desert us for Rome?'

'He is loyal to the Queen and has no Catholic beliefs, my Lord, I am certain of that.' Nor any other, I might have added, but that would have caused trouble of a different order.

Lord Burghley turned to William Davison. 'Fetch the prisoners.'

He seated himself at the head of the long table, signifying to Thomas Walsingham to join him. The two whispered together. Frizer and I were not invited to sit and remained standing to one side. William returned with three soldiers wearing swords and carrying cudgels, leading Christopher and the man Gifford Gilbert on a rope. The prisoners' hands were tied before them and they were tied to each other. The soldier holding the rope led them through the door and then jerked them to a halt at the far end of the table, causing them to stumble against each other. Gifford, a small, older man with a grey beard and little hair, wore dirty grey worsted and looked like a man pulled from a shipwreck. Christopher wore a black tunic of good quality but it was torn and stained, his stockings were holed and one of his shoes was losing its sole, slapping on the floorboards as he walked. His hair was matted and untidy, his beard unkempt. He looked tired, resentful, defiant.

William Davison had returned with more papers than before and now hurried to Lord Burghley's side, whispering in his ear. These new papers evidently did not concern the prisoners because there was a protracted pause while he and Lord Burghley shuffled through them, William taking instructions. Recalling Robert Cecil's urging me to ensure that Christopher spoke respectfully, I walked over to him. I half expected the soldiers to obstruct me but they stepped aside. His brown eyes met mine as I approached and he smiled, sardonically I thought. He had lost a tooth since we last met. Both men stank of gaol.

'Thomas, I am honoured. How is Mrs Phelippes?'

'She is well, I thank you. I have a—'

'I am heartily glad to hear it.' There was something aggressive in his tone, as if he were trying to keep me at bay. 'But truly I am, And you too, I trust,' he added, more softly.

'I have a message from Sir Robert.' All the others were listening but there was nothing for it but to go on. 'His Lordship is inclined to be understanding, provided you are contrite.'

The man Gifford, who was staring pleadingly at me, nodded with unexpected vigour. 'We are, sir, we are. Truly.' His voice was hoarsened to a croak.

'Contrition?' Christopher's sardonic smile returned. 'That is the coin of our payment?'

'That or your lives.'

'So?' His glance was challenging. 'Or, as God wills, as you might put it?'

At that moment we were joined by Thomas Walsingham

and Frizer. 'Speak sweetly and all shall be well,' Thomas whispered to Christopher.

'Humble pie, Kit,' said Frizer. 'Time you learned the taste of it.' He spoke in a joshing manner, grinning.

Christopher looked as if he were about to respond in some other way but swallowed it and turned to Thomas. 'Is Baines here?'

'He is. His Lordship will hear him first.'

William Davison collected his papers and, at a nod from Lord Burghley, marched down beside the table past us and towards the door. 'About to start,' he whispered.

The prisoners and soldiers remained where they were, Thomas resumed his seat and Frizer and I stood to the side. While we waited Lord Burghley conversed quietly again with Thomas until the door opened and William reappeared with Richard Baines.

I had not seen him before but I knew much about him. He was a plump man with a fair beard, well dressed and well fed by that stage of his life, though he had not always been. He was quick in speech and wrote as copiously and fluently in Latin as in English. My work had made me more familiar with his hand than he could have guessed. Like Christopher, he was another Cambridge man once suspected by the authorities there of having gone to Rheims to become a priest in order to return England and further the Catholic cause. Unlike Christopher, who had been working for us, he really had gone to Rheims and really had become a priest. But while there he had secretly resolved to work against the Pope and the English Catholic exiles. He raised discontent among other young recruits and even plotted to poison their water, like the Jew in Christopher's play. He wrote descriptions of his fellows and their plans which he contrived by indirect means to have delivered into the hands of Mr Secretary, who sent him money for them. He thus became, in his own opinion, one of our agents.

But he never was, in Mr Secretary's eyes. We had a number of such volunteers, freelancers of the intelligence world who offered their services. Some were useful but often they were not, being men who in their own estimation played a great part in affairs of which they knew less than they thought. In particular, they did not know who else might be fishing in their pool, more discreetly than they.

Having become a priest, Baines was about to return to England in order, so far as his masters in Rheims were concerned, to work secretly against us. But really, he claimed, to work secretly for us against them. However, he was arrested before he could leave Rheims and after some little torture wrote a fulsome confession which was published, securing him his pardon and permission to return to England.

He and Christopher must have taken against each other soon after meeting for not only did he denounce Christopher and Gilbert to the governor of Flushing but at the time of Christopher's death he wrote the infamous note I told you of. You will remember that this denounced Christopher for, among other crimes, 'his damnable judgement of religion and his scorn of God's word'. Later, I discovered it was Baines, not

Thomas Kyd, who first said that Christopher persuaded men to atheism. It was also he who denounced the innocent Kyd for the Dutch Church libel. This worthy man of God did it for money and the terms of his denunciations are so like the terms of his own confession that I conclude he had a sheath of phrases, all feathered and sharpened, to be shot from his bow at anyone he took against, or from whom money was to be made. After he converted to our own church he was rewarded with a comfortable living in Lincolnshire.

But the malice of Baines's writings was not evident in his person that morning. He was modest and respectful, answering Lord Burghley's questions with frequent Your Lordships, Your Honours, By Your Honour's Leaves and If Please Your Honours. None of which entertained or impressed Lord Burghley. Having got Baines to confirm the report of the governor of Flushing – *viz.* that Christopher had provoked Gilbert into making and uttering the forged Dutch shilling, with the intention of making many more before fleeing to the seminary at Rheims – Lord Burghley then said with quiet precision, 'But the two accused contradict you. Gilbert the goldsmith says you and Marlowe urged him to forge the shilling equally and Marlowe says it was you who planned to utter more coins and flee to Rheims, your former home.' He turned to Christopher and Gilbert. 'Is that not so?'

He made it sound as if he had already taken statements from the accused. There was surprise on Gilbert's face as well as fear and for a moment he merely gazed, his toothless mouth open. Then he nodded. 'It is so, my Lord, it is so.'

I feared at first that Christopher wouldn't reply. For a second or two he returned Lord Burghley's uncompromising gaze, then he turned to face Baines. 'It is so, my Lord,' he said clearly.

Baines was about to protest but Lord Burghley cut him short. 'Two against one. What have you to say to that?'

'It is not so, my Lord, I—'

'And only one Dutch shilling uttered. No coin of this realm. And no more were made. Do you agree?'

'My Lord, their – his, Marlowe's – intention was—'

'What you say it was. Or not. And yours was what he says it was. Or not.'

'But the port and town of Flushing are English. Therefore the utterance of counterfeit coin—'

'Of a *foreign* coin is rightly a matter for the governor to deal with as he thinks fit. He has the necessary powers. It is not for us to consider here. There need be no trial.' He turned to William. 'You will write to the governor and tell him that I want no more such minor vexations referred to me. We deal daily in weightier matters.' He turned back to Baines. 'I do not wish to see you here again without better purpose. If I do your stay may be prolonged.' He turned again to William. 'See that the prisoners are released. Now begone, all of you.'

And so we and the case were dismissed. Thomas Walsingham, Frizer and I left the palace with Christopher. Gilbert disappeared. Whether he lived in London or Flushing or elsewhere I know not. Most of us are like fishes in the lives of others, a silvery flank glimpsed once and never seen again. As we shuffled out it was clear that Baines did not want to leave with us but at the same time feared to irritate his Lordship by lingering. He compromised by following ten feet behind. Christopher paid him no attention at all but Frizer twice turned and grinned, which made him pause until we drew ahead.

'Mangy dog,' Frizer said. 'Chuck a stone and he'd yelp. Bark at him, Kit, see him run.'

But Christopher ignored him. We stood talking in the street outside Whitehall Palace until Thomas and Frizer left for Thomas's manor in Chislehurst. Christopher said he would return to the lodging he had taken after leaving Mary's.

'If I still have it. I have been away longer than promised and someone else may have taken it.'

'Come to my house. You can wash and borrow clean clothes.'

He nodded. We watched Baines hurry across the road towards the Abbey. 'Good riddance,' I said. 'He has it in for you.'

'He has it in for everyone, chiefly himself. He cannot accept the failure he senses he is and cannot bear that others should be better.'

'Why did you do it, coining that shilling?'

'Boredom, curiosity. And maybe future gain, who knows? If it had worked it would be comforting to know that in time of need one could make money, actually make it.'

'So you were prepared to do it, to go coining?'

'Prepared, but not doing it. Prepared to do anything, Thomas, as you know. Or nothing.'

'You do not care what you do?'

'I should like to know the limits, the limits of what I am capable of. It's those that define what we are.'

'We know what we are, surely?'

'But not what we may be.' By this time we were walking back towards the Strand and he was looking down as if reading a script in the dirt. 'We all feel we are at the centre of our circle, the circle that is us. But it's our boundaries that make us what we are. It's the line, the boundary, that makes the circle. Draw it differently and the centre is moved and we are different. Take away that line, that boundary, and what is left? A being capable of becoming anything, depending on where the line is drawn. And if you are unsure where your own line, your own boundary, is – if you can't feel it or sense it – does that mean you are capable of anything? Could we all be saints? Or Tamburlaine? Or anything?'

'Well, and so what?'

He stopped in the street and clapped me on the shoulder, pulling me round to face him. 'Thomas, that is precisely it. So what? So nothing. And if nothing, what matters? Why does anything matter?'

We had discussed this before, of course, and it always left me discomforted. It seemed to me that many things mattered, if not to us, then to God. But he would not accept that. Whatever I said he would respond with – why? Why does that matter? Why? Show me. Show how it matters whether we exist or not. He perhaps sensed my thinking because he continued for me.

'We think things matter because they matter to God. But if there is no God, then there is nothing to make anything matter beyond what we choose to say matters. But how can saying something matters make it so? We could just as easily say something else – anything else – matters. This not that, apples not pears, with no better and no worse reason.'

'I hope you do not write such heresy in your plays.'

'Of course not. Not obviously, anyway. Or I should not be alive to shock you with it now.'

'So being alive matters?'

We were walking on by then but he stopped again. '*Touché*. We all feel that being alive matters. Yet when I am dead it cannot matter to me that I am dead, and when those who mourn me are dead – those blessed few – it can matter to no one. It matters to me only because I am alive and want to go on living, just like any horse or dog or rat. But what, apart from that, makes anything matter? Why be good? Why be moral? Why be anything? Because God wills, you would say. But if there is no God—'

'Keep your voice down or you will have us both burned.' The Strand was as busy as always, with boats unloading, men shouting and dogs everywhere. We were bumped and jostled. 'Where do you find such ideas? Where have you read them?'

'Nowhere, no one dare write them. They come from talk.'

'Talk with Ralegh and his friends? Your name has been

mentioned with free-thinkers. You should be careful what you say.'

'Well informed as ever, Thomas. Everything comes to you eventually.'

'Ralegh has powerful enemies at Court. Lord Essex and he are at daggers drawn, you know that? And Robert Cecil is wary of him, so he has no ally there. He has spoken in parliament against the government on the matter of immigrants and seems likely to rouse the common people. You should choose your friends more carefully.'

Christopher's particular friends? No, sir, I do not know who his particular friends were. I was not part of his world, as I have said. Watson must have been one but he was a dying man at the time I am speaking of. Thomas Walsingham latterly, yes, he was probably a particular friend. They must have seen more of each other than I knew, as you shall hear.

Christopher stayed that night at my house, his first good sleep, he said, since arrest in the Netherlands. He talked with Mary that day and he and I talked again before he left the next morning, but I cannot recall it. I don't think we continued our Strand conversation. He may have talked about the theatre and plays, although he had been away from them for a while. I remember he bade farewell to Mary most tenderly. I do not recall our parting, which is a sadness to me.

Chapter Ten

Forgive me, sir, but I know little of Christopher's friendship with Thomas Walsingham apart from the fact that they became close in the last year or two of his life. Sir Thomas was a great admirer of Christopher's verses and invited him to stay at Scadbury whenever the plague was in London and the theatres closed, as they were by the early summer of 1593. The last night of his life was spent there. They probably discussed poetry and play-making, Thomas and his wife having a great interest in the arts, though it couldn't have been all art because Frizer was there too. Christopher spent much of those days sitting out by the moat and writing a long poem, Thomas told me afterwards.

You ask whether I was a particular friend of Christopher's. I am not sure what you mean but since our friendship was unique, perhaps yes. I am sure he had no other like it, given the way we met and his involvement in our secret work. I think he felt protective of me – as I of him for different reasons – despite his being the younger man and far less intimate with matters of state than I was. Despite, too, the differences between us over religious belief. Or perhaps because of them. His thinking shocked me but I think he sensed that, despite myself, I was tempted to follow him into the snows of thought where no God walks. Tempted, but I lacked his courage to follow where Reason leads. He sensed that too and handled me softly, as I have said. It is easy for the young to be extreme in belief or love or hate, but less common to be gentle, which he always was with me despite his fiery reputation.

He was gentle with Mary, too, very gentle. I would say theirs was a particular friendship. I am sure he was fond of her, as I know she was of him. And, though it pains me to say it, I daresay she would have married him if he had asked. He had the gift of intimacy, to which women responded. But he seemed no more uxorious, as he himself put it, than he was possessive. His warmth and generosity were the other side of the coin of impatience and impetuosity. He came to our wedding and gave Mary a poem he had written, with sentiments so tender that she wept. I cannot recall it and have not seen it these many years but I am sure she has it somewhere. Later, when our first child was still-born, he came and sat with Mary. God has not blessed us with children, as you perhaps know, sir. Two others were still-born later. But that was after Christopher was dead.

No, I did not see him killed. I was not there. But, yes, it is true that I viewed the place where he was killed, the room. That was some time afterwards when I was tasked by Sir Robert Cecil with investigating the events, discreetly. As for what happened and how it came about, I can tell you only what others said. Since you seem to know the facts well enough I doubt I can add greatly to your knowledge. But if His Majesty wishes . . .

Very well. Christopher was killed on the thirtieth day of May in the year of our Lord 1593. It was a bad time to be in London. The warm weather brought with it the plague that claimed, if I remember rightly, some two thousand souls. Food and produce became scarce and there was much discontent among the poorer parts, as well as among apprentices and journeymen. They also resented the great numbers of Protestant traders who had fled from Catholic oppression in France, Belgium and the Netherlands. Unruly mobs made the streets more dangerous than usual and Mary and I would have left the city for our properties in Essex or Yorkshire but that I needed employment to pay for their upkeep, Mr Secretary being almost three years dead.

At Easter the tension in the streets was increased by anonymous placards and notices threatening violence to foreigners. It was claimed they took business from our traders and had more rights from the Queen than the ordinary English. The Privy Council was alarmed and a secret commission was formed to discover the anonymous writers and printers who were fuelling these flames. Thanks to Sir Robert Cecil, William Waad and I were appointed to it. This was welcome new work and I remember saying to Mary that it justified our decision to remain in London during the plague.

Then, early in May, our task was made more urgent by

the Dutch Church libel, which I believe I have mentioned already? It was a ballad threatening violence against strangers, nailed one night to the wall of the Dutch Church yard in Broad Street. Forgotten now like most great matters, it was a mighty concern at the time and our commission was ordered to find the culprits forthwith. The first and most obvious clues pointed to Christopher because the ballad was signed 'Tamburlaine', which of course reminded everyone of his play. The second clue was lines about the Machiavellian machinations of Jewish merchants, which echoed another of his plays, *The Jew of Malta*, performed only the previous year. Added to this, it was said that Christopher himself praised the political writings of Machiavelli. He never did to me but I can believe it – he relished uncomfortable realities, especially the realities of power. Yet other lines in the ballad referred to the St Bartholomew's Eve massacre in Paris in terms that echoed Christopher's most recent play, *The Massacre at Paris*, played earlier that same year to great acclaim. It showed Protestants being massacred in their churches by Catholic mobs and the ballad threatened that English mobs would do the same to foreigners in their churches in London. The Privy Council promised a reward of a hundred crowns to anyone who informed on the writers. Anyone refusing to talk could be put to the torture in Bridewell without further authorisation.

In fact, Christopher himself never became a suspect since the commission accepted that he would not have signed the ballad Tamburlaine or referred to his own plays unless he wanted to be discovered, in which case he would have used his own name. One or two on the commission wanted him listed as suspect anyway but William Waad and I carried the argument.

However, as I have told you already, another play-maker, Thomas Kyd, was arrested and put to the torture after being denounced by Richard Baines. He was the son of a printer and therefore, it was argued, knew how to put such leaflets together. I am afraid I went along with this, on the words of others. But as his torture progressed and he continued protesting his innocence, while blaming Christopher for the heretical papers found among his own, William Waad and I grew ever more doubtful and eventually persuaded the commission to release him. But not before he had suffered grievously.

The papers Kyd attributed to Christopher were three pages of a theological disputation in which the divinity of Christ was denied, arguing that He was wholly human and not at all divine. This – I am sure you will know, sir – is the Unitarian or Arian heresy, arguments for which had been published, examined and confuted many years before. But in those fevered times they were seen as atheistical and dangerous. Kyd defended himself by saying that Christopher's papers must have been shuffled among his when they shared a room. This was credible, since that was the kind of argument Christopher enjoyed. And not only he – many true and Godly theologians have described and disputed such heresies.

But I had underestimated the fever of those times, the

lust for conspiracy and heresy. Pleased to be back in harness and doing the state's service, I had naively assumed that all would be as in Mr Secretary's day. Although a forward Salvationist, he was a pragmatist whose nose told him when too much enthusiasm threatened the workings of the state. He would stamp upon Protestants as hard as upon Catholics. But in these new times competing hands tugged on the tiller of the state and Kyd's papers were taken as confirming what Kyd and Robert Greene and Richard Baines said about Christopher's provocations and his association with Ralegh and the free-thinkers. Lord Essex's faction still saw Ralegh as a rival and used any weapon to attack him or anyone associated with him. At the same time, Lord Burghley and Robert Cecil would not defend Ralegh because of the trouble he caused in parliament by opposing Protestant immigration.

Thus was I summoned again by Sir Robert Cecil to my old perch in the New Library. He used it, he told me, for discreet meetings because few knew of it and fewer still were allowed in. Theoretically, the Earl of Essex had access, as I have said, but he disdained it as not a grand enough stage for his appearances. Besides, he had no fondness for books and maps. Robert Cecil smiled his thin small smile as he told me that, which I took to be a reference to the Earl's military misadventures. But that was after we had done our business.

He began by asking whether I had heard anything of or from the Earl of Essex or any of his circle since the coining business. 'They know you and Thomas Walsingham were there and spoke in Marlowe's favour,' he said. 'Have you seen anything of Nicholas Skeres or Ingram Frizer?'

'No, sir. I know Skeres wears the Earl's livery but Frizer—'

'Frizer is rumoured to be associated with the Earl's party, perhaps via Skeres. Have you seen him since the examination?' I had not and didn't know he was associated with the Earl. 'He may not be. In fact, my hunch is that he is not. He is Thomas Walsingham's man and probably loyal. But Skeres is very much of the Earl's party. Have you seen Robert Poley?'

'No, sir.'

'Skeres and Frizer are very thick with him.'

'With Poley it is never easy to tell—'

'I know, I know.' He stared at the globe which had been so beloved of Mr Secretary. But he did not turn or touch it, as Mr Secretary was wont, meditatively, with his fingertips. He simply sat with his hands flat upon the desk and his eyes on the great sea. Then he turned to me. 'You have dealt in secrets many years, Mr Phelippes. You were trusted by Sir Francis as few men were. I am now going to tell you another secret, one as great as any you have known.' He paused again. 'I would like your assurance that you will keep it close.'

'You have it, sir.'

'And you understand the consequences if you do not?'

I did.

'We are preparing the succession.'

Even now, sir, after these many years and when everything Sir Robert plotted has come about, I feel the hairs on my neck prick when I recall those words. The succession to Queen

Elizabeth, her lack of an heir, was an arrow in the eye of all her privy counsellors throughout her reign. It had caused the death of a queen and was the subject of plots and speculations throughout Europe, not to mention the executions that flowed from it within this realm. Although she was well aware of it, the succession problem could not even be mentioned to Her Majesty. She would hear nothing of it, would not acknowledge the possibility that she might not reign forever. It was dangerous even to think of it, in fact treason to discuss it. Yet Robert Cecil did with me that day in May.

'The Queen will die,' he said, 'if not tomorrow, the day after, this year, next year, ten years hence. But die she will. If we do nothing there will be confusion, civil war, invasion and the settlement we have built these last forty years will be gone. Our only hope of peaceful succession is James VI, King of Scotland. He and the Queen share blood. That was why we had to execute his mother and why we must now have him on the throne. He covets the English crown as well as his own. We know that. He will overlook the execution of his mother in return for the throne.'

You understand, sir, that these were not my words but Sir Robert's? I would not wish King James to think that I spoke of him in such manner. And I know, of course – I know to my cost – that he was not prepared to overlook his mother's execution entirely.

Well, Sir Robert then told me firmly that no proposals had been made, nothing definite said, the succession not even mentioned, but there was secret correspondence between the two Courts, an agreement on the need for mutual understanding and for a reliable, discreet channel of communication. 'Her Majesty knows nothing of this,' he said. 'But she is shrewd, she is bound to suspect. She prefers not to know but trusts us to see to it while ensuring that nothing ever, ever is known of it. If it comes out, heads will roll.'

That was not a figure of speech. Messages between the two Courts were carried by Robert Poley, who had certain business of his own with certain Scottish gentlemen and so an ostensible reason for journeying there. He did not know what he conveyed, though he knew enough to know it was more than his life's worth to breathe a word that he conveyed anything. And so far he had not. 'At least, I think he has not,' said Sir Robert softly. 'Twice we have sent your friend Marlowe with him, to keep an eye on him. Of course, Marlowe knows nothing of what is going on, either, but he reported nothing untoward, no unexplained contacts or absences on Poley's part. But we have learned through other sources that the Earl of Essex has also his own secret channel to the Scottish Court. We do not know what passes along it but we can be sure it will be more to Essex's benefit than the state's. King James is cautious and will no doubt play along with it until he sees which of these opposing English factions is likely to triumph. We believe Essex knows nothing of our activities. If he finds it out he will whisper it in the Queen's ear within the hour and it will be the end for us. She continues to indulge him.'

Meanwhile, he worried that Poley might be tempted to ride

two horses. He was seeing ever more of Skeres and others of Essex's circle, sometimes Frizer too. 'I suspect it is some nefarious business of his own, something they are cooking up between them. But I cannot be sure and until I am I dare not risk using him again. What I want of you, Mr Phelippes, is that you insert your friend Marlowe into that little group, get him close with them, find out whether it is business of their own they meet about – and if so what – or whether Poley is negotiating with the Earl through Skeres. Do you still trust Marlowe, and would he do it?'

I had not seen Christopher for some time. I doubted he would want to take time away from the theatre to play games with Poley and the others, for whom he had no great fondness.

'He journeyed to Scotland with Poley willingly enough on our behalf when the theatres were closed,' Sir Robert added. 'They are closed again now with the plague. He must be at a loose end and he will need money.'

'But would I not have to tell him what to look out for, tell him about the Earl and about—'

'No. You simply tell him you want him to find out what Poley, Skeres and Frizer are cooking between them. He has no reason to ask why but if he does you may tell him you are with me and that you are worried that Poley might be getting closer to Essex. Emphasise that he could use this time when the theatres are closed to earn himself some good money by insinuating himself deeper into their company. He should be glad of the chance.'

I wasn't so sure, suspecting that Christopher was now too

busy and successful in his own world to have much time for ours. But his trips to Scotland with Poley – which I had not known about – suggested some willingness. I would of course have agreed anyway, but when Cecil suggested that I too would be well rewarded for my help and my silence, I thanked him.

I should explain, sir, that earlier that year I was briefly imprisoned for my debts to the Crown and then released thanks to Lord Buckhurst, who petitioned the Queen for me. This meant that I had lost touch with Christopher who was by then with Lord Strange's players at the Rose theatre. The theatres now being closed, I did not know where he lodged nor where else to find him. I tried the Rose first. Most of the company were dispersed but a few players were still there, offering fencing lessons to any who came by, including me. They had not seen Christopher for some time and did not know where he lodged. It was clear they were finding it hard to put food into their mouths so I gave them a shilling and promised more if Christopher called and they sent him to my house.

At home I told Mary everything. Sir Robert Cecil would have been appalled that I should share state secrets with my wife, given how many wives love to gossip, but Mary was discreet and I trusted her with all my business, as I still do. It was as well I did because she immediately told me that Christopher lodged in a house at the far end of Hog's Lane, not far from her own house which we had let since our marriage.

'How do you know?'

'He called. He called last week.'

'Here? He was here? You never told me.'

'He has never ceased calling, all the time you were in prison. He was concerned for me.'

I half realised what a dullard I must be, wrapped up in my own world. For a moment I doubted her, remembering how well they got on and feeling again the jealousy I had felt before we married. 'What do you do when he calls?'

'We talk. We always have. That is all.' She took my hand and stood close, smiling. 'Thomas, you have no need to worry. I am as faithful a wife as you are a husband.'

If that were true, there really was no need to worry. I was persuaded of it, yet I couldn't help going on. 'What do you talk about?'

'Everything and nothing. Besides, I don't think he is looking for a wife. Or mistress. He is too busy for such distractions.'

'He can't be now with the theatres closed.'

'He is writing poetry. He read me some.'

'He reads you poetry?'

'Yes, why not? I am sure he would read it to you, if you liked it. But you always say you do not.'

I left it at that.

His lodgings were above a baker's and luckily he was in. He had a long room with two windows and beneath each a table covered with papers. He shared, he said, with another player who was away with part of the company, touring in

Oxfordshire and Gloucestershire until the theatres reopened. Christopher was writing at one of the tables and showed no surprise at seeing me.

'You turn up like a bad penny, Thomas, whenever I have time on my hands.'

'A good penny this time, I hope. Maybe many a penny.'

'Always welcome. How is dear Mary?'

We talked of this and that for a while. He said living above the baker's meant the house was always warm but that he and the other player were always tired because they were woken in the early hours by the baker and, unlike him, were not in bed before the day was out.

No, I fear I cannot recall anything of the player he shared with. I'm not sure I ever knew anything about him. I've a faint thought that it may have been the player I met once, the one who was also a play-maker and with whom he collaborated. But I don't know why I think that. It may have been from something he said.

I told him my business, without of course mentioning negotiations with the Scottish Court. He did not react with his usual enthusiasm. 'But how am I to insinuate myself in that tight little triangle of Poley, Skeres and Frizer? I never see Poley unless Sir Robert Cecil sends me to accompany him to Scotland with letters. Skeres I have not seen since the Babington affair, which is no loss at all, and Frizer – well, we see a bit of each other now that he is servant to Thomas Walsingham, as you know. Thomas himself I see but since the plague came he stays at Scadbury, his manor in Chislehurst.

Wisely. The plague cart picked up two more bodies from Hog's Lane this morning.'

'I saw it on my way here. Could you seek refuge with Thomas at Scadbury while the plague lasts? He would welcome you, surely, especially if you wanted to write verses there.'

'It would mean sharing a roof with Frizer. Maybe even a room.'

'Then you would know if he meets Poley and Skeres.'

He agreed after more talk, partly because he liked the idea of escaping London for a while and was intrigued by my suggestion that Poley might be planning change horses to ride with Essex. But he doubted it. 'Not because he would have any compunction about changing sides, but I doubt he would see it to his advantage. He once said to me that Essex was a firework, bright and unpredictable, liable to go off at any time and then be finished, but that Burghley and Cecil were a trail of powder, carefully laid. I think he'll stick with them.'

'Nevertheless, I should like to be able to tell Robert Cecil what they meet and talk about, whatever it is.'

'It will be money, money matters.' He nodded, smiling to himself. 'I'd bet you a guinea on it if you were a betting man.'

That was the last time I saw him alive.

CHAPTER ELEVEN

Christopher left for Scadbury the following day. He was to send me reports and I would reply by letter to a local inn. In fact, he had little to report during his brief time there. Sir Thomas and Lady Walsingham made him welcome, urging him to stay as long as he wished and providing him with a spacious chamber in which to write a long poem he was working on. He did not have to share with Ingram Frizer, who had become steward to the Walsinghams and was now part of the household. Frizer was less welcoming, of course, but not hostile. Or not outrightly so. 'We rub along,' Christopher wrote. It was in the interest of neither that there should be obvious friction between them and there was no sign that Frizer suspected Christopher's motive for being there. Although there were indications that he was jealous of Christopher's intimacy with Sir Thomas. Presumably he feared that Christopher could influence Thomas against him.

Meanwhile, there was no sign of any plotting with Poley and Skeres. Christopher learned only that Skeres was somewhere in London and that he and Frizer were involved in property business, as Frizer called it, while Poley was said to be abroad. Christopher made an effort to talk business with Frizer and they agreed they should all meet when Poley returned.

I was summoned again by Sir Robert Cecil. He told me that Poley was in the Low Countries on government business and would return soon. Christopher was to be sure to meet him whether or not the other two were there. Meanwhile, I was to warn Christopher that a warrant was about to be issued for his apprehension. He was not to worry – he was not a suspect, nor was it anything to do with the Dutch Church libel, though it arose from it. It was part of the Essex faction's manoeuvres against Ralegh, whom they hoped to indict for heresy and free-thinking. Sir Robert had been able to see to it that Christopher was summoned only as a witness, not as party to the alleged crimes, and that he would not be imprisoned, merely required to be available to report regularly to the Privy Council for so long as necessary. In fact, Sir Robert was confident that he could so arrange it that Christopher was never called, even if the case was brought. But it was important that he showed himself to be cooperative, neither resisting nor absconding. I was to ensure he did that by writing to him that day.

On 18 May – I have these latter dates by heart as a result of my subsequent investigation – Henry Maunder, one of the Queen's Messengers, set out for Scadbury with a warrant to apprehend Christopher and bring him before the Privy Council. On 20 May Christopher accompanied Henry

Maunder – I believe they knew each other anyway – back to the Council, then sitting at Greenwich as the Queen was there. It was eight or nine miles from Scadbury and Christopher appeared before the Council later that day, which on receipt of his indemnity commanded him to appear daily before them until licensed to the contrary.

They were still gathering evidence, I later discovered, part of which was another note by Richard Baines listing Christopher's alleged blasphemies and heresies. I also later discovered that Baines was put up to it by a pair of rogues, Thomas Drury and Richard Cholmeley, servants to the Earl of Essex. Why Baines was so keen to help them, having already done his worst to damage Christopher in Flushing, I know not. Personal malice, most likely, fuelled by money. Yet I never knew Christopher bear malice towards Baines; he showed only disdain or indifference. Perhaps that was enough. Indifference can be more wounding than darts of dislike or arrows of hate.

Meanwhile our inquiry into the Dutch Church libel had widened into a hunt for any malcontents who tried to raise the mob against foreigners and the government. It was not our business to enquire into individual heresies and so I could show no interest in the case involving Christopher. I had news of it only from him or from Sir Robert, both infrequent. My last communication from Christopher was a note saying that Poley was expected within a day or two, depending on weather, and that he was to meet him with Skeres and Frizer to discuss 'business matters'.

What happened next is a matter of official record, as you must know, sir. I presume you have access to the record?

Very well. You will have read that on 30 May Christopher Marlowe, Ingram Frizer, Nicholas Skeres and Robert Poley met on Deptford Strand, on the Thames in Kent, at the house of Eleanor Bull, a respectable widow who was distant cousin to Lord Burghley. Mrs Bull let rooms to gentlemen requiring rest or sustenance while waiting to embark or recovering from the rigours of a voyage. Poley had taken rooms the day before when he returned from the Low Countries. He intended to stay two or three days, having despatches to deliver to the Court at nearby Greenwich.

The four men met at ten in the morning in one of the upstairs rooms taken by Poley, who must either have already delivered his despatches or was in no hurry to do so. I have among my papers here a copy of the coroner's account of what happened in that room. If you wish I can read it to you, sir. I shall leave out the names of jurors and other legal details. But you must forgive my slowness. My eyes are going and even with these extra candles produced for your visit it is not easy reading.

The coroner of the Queen's household was then William Danby and it fell to him to conduct the inquest because Christopher was killed within the verge of the Court, the Queen residing as I have said at nearby Greenwich. Having named the four men present in the upstairs room, Danby records:

. . . the aforesaid in the said County of Kent within the
verge, about the tenth hour before noon of the same day, met
together in a room in the house of a certain Eleanor Bull,
widow; & there passed the time together & dined & after
dinner were in quiet sort together there & walked in the
garden belonging to the said house until the sixth hour after
noon of the same day & then returned from the said garden
to the room aforesaid and there together and in company
supped; and after supper the said Ingram & Christopher
Morley were in speech & uttered one to the other divers
malicious words for the reason that they could not be at one
nor agree about the payment of the sum of pence, that is le
reckonynge, *there;*

I'm sure there is no need to remind you, sir, of the history of
relations between Christopher and Ingram Frizer. It began
in enmity and, though afterwards they affected a cheerful
familiarity necessitated by being parties to common endeav-
ours, they were never of like mind. As I said, there were
rumours they were rivals over a wench, though I never knew
Christopher engaged with a woman. Nor a man, come to that,
as some suggested. Though there is, as I have oft told you,
much I do not know.

Well, yes, perhaps there was some rivalry for the affec-
tions of Sir Thomas Walsingham, but their dislike of each
other existed before that. Some dogs fight on meeting,
with no cause apparent. It is in their temperaments. But
Christopher was not a man to bear grudges. His nature

was fundamentally generous, he would ignore rather than pursue. Look how he shrugged off Baines. Granted, he could lash out in temper, as you know, but he could also be fond and sympathetic. He was with Mary and, in a different key, with me. He mocked more than he hated, which a man like Frizer would have found hard to bear.

As you have just heard, William Danby wrote that the cause of their argument that day was the reckoning, Eleanor Bull's bill. There is no reason to doubt that, it could easily have been sufficient cause. Poley, Frizer and Skeres were all sharp with money, Frizer and Skeres being notable cozeners, as you know. Christopher was what you might call careful with money and, though I never knew him engage in fraud, I came to suspect there might have been more to his interest in coining in Flushing than the casual experiment he claimed. Yet he must have been prosperous when he died, his plays being so popular. You might think he would disdain to fight over the cost of a meal or two, but perhaps that takes too little account of feelings between him and Frizer. The real red meat of an argument is not always the cause given.

William Danby goes on to write:

& the said Christopher Morley then lying upon a bed in the room where they supped, & moved with anger against the said Ingram ffrysar upon the words as aforesaid spoken between them, And the said Ingram then and there sitting in the room aforesaid with his back towards the bed where the said Christopher Morley was then lying, sitting near

*the bed, that is, <u>nere the bed,</u> & with the front part of his
body towards the table & the aforesaid Nicholas Skeres &
Robert Poley sitting on either side of the said Ingram in
such a manner that the same Ingram ffrysar in no wise
could take flight: it so befell that the said Christopher
Morley on a sudden and of his malice towards the said
Ingram aforethought, then & there maliciously drew the
dagger of the said Ingram which was at his back, and with
the same dagger the said Christopher Morley then & there
maliciously gave the said Ingram two wounds on his head
of the length of two inches and of the depth of a quarter of
an inch; whereupon the said Ingram, in fear of being slain,
& sitting in the manner aforesaid between the said Nicholas
Skeres & Robert Poley so that he could not in anywise get
away from the said Christopher Morley; and so it befell
in that affray that the said Ingram, in defence of his life,
with the dagger aforesaid of the value of 12d. gave the said
Christopher then and there a mortal wound over his right
eye to the depth of two inches & of the width of one inch; of
which mortal wound the aforesaid Christopher Morley then
& there instantly died;*

There you have it, sir. That is the record. I believe it is essentially what happened. There is no reason to assert otherwise.
But I can add to it somewhat, not only through what I have
already told you about how Christopher came to be there, but
through my subsequent investigations on behalf of Sir Robert.

I continued in his employ for some time following the

finding that Frizer had killed in self-defence and his subsequent pardoning, as had happened some years before with Thomas Watson and Christopher. Sir Robert still wanted to know what they discussed that day, to be as sure as possible that Poley was not swinging to Essex. He tasked me with questioning each of them.

Naturally, he wanted it done without alerting them to his interest, if possible without mentioning him or Essex. 'Do it as one grieving for the loss of your friend,' he said. 'He was after all the man who introduced you to your wife. They know of your official relations with him, of course, but those are far in the past. You admire his verses, you wish to compose a memorial to him, to commemorate your friendship.'

There was in fact truth in that, as perhaps you have sensed, sir. I feel his loss still. He was a presence in my life like no other. It affected Mary grievously, she wept for days. Only when he was gone did I realise how often I engaged in an imaginary dialogue with him, questioning, arguing, construing his responses. His Kentish burr was ever in my head, querying my opinions, teasing me for my judgements. Thus do we keep the dead alive, giving them life after death. They live in us.

How did I hear of it? Late, the news reached me late, he was dead and buried before I heard anything of it. Few knew of our connection, I suppose, and those that did probably thought of it as a professional relation, not a friendship. I had it from Nicholas Faunt who had run into Poley after the inquest. Nicholas, like many of us who had served Mr

Secretary, was seeking employ and called at my house because he had heard I was sometimes engaged by Sir Robert Cecil and wished me to mention him.

'Please assure him I am of sound Puritan stock, a Canterbury man and a scholar of Corpus Christi, Cambridge,' he said. 'A lineage trusted by Mr Secretary and now by Sir Robert, too, I have heard. Though we are one fewer now, Robert Poley tells me.'

'A defection?'

'No, a death. The actor or play-maker who did some work for us in Mr Secretary's time. You knew him. Morely or Marley or some such name.'

'Christopher? Christopher Marlowe?'

'The very man. Killed brawling, Poley said. But, tell me, are you much engaged with Sir Robert? Does he heed what you say? I would serve him as I did Mr Secretary, if he would have me.'

I was too shaken to heed much of what else Nicholas said. He had not asked Poley for details, being more concerned with gaining a position for himself. All he could add was that Poley too was engaged with Sir Robert and worried that his involvement in the brawl might prejudice his reputation for discreet behaviour.

Later, I did mention Nicholas Faunt to Sir Robert, who did engage him. Nicholas served him well, I believe, gaining in discretion as he gained in years.

As for my own discreet enquiries on Sir Robert's behalf, I started with Frizer, calling on him at Scadbury one fine July day. He had spent most of June in prison until pardoned by the court. Sir Robert contrived reason for me to visit, sending me with letters for Sir Thomas. The carp in the moat were basking in the sun and Sir Thomas was conveniently out hunting, which meant I had to wait and had time with Frizer alone. He said, of course, that I could leave the letters with him but I said my orders were to hand them over in person. I tried to flatter him by adding that otherwise I should have been happy to, since Sir Thomas obviously trusted him in matters of business, but that I thought these letters concerned Court appointments which the Court officials who appointed me wanted kept close.

Frizer therefore knew I still had important connections and so was wary enough to be civil, which was not always his natural state. 'I was very sad to hear of Marlowe's death,' I said. 'He was a friend I much miss, despite his sudden temper. And it must have been fearful for you. You must have feared for your life in those moments.'

We were sitting with mugs of ale on a bench in the sun, overlooking the moat. He took a long draught and shook his head. 'No time to fear. He was onto me like a cat, pounding my head before I knew what was happening.'

'Lucky you were not more grievously injured. He could have cut your throat or stuck the knife in your neck.'

'He could've, easy, which is why I don't think that was his intent. He pounded and pummelled, as I told the coroner, using the pommel of my own dagger to give me these cuts. You can still feel them here, see.' He turned the back of his head towards me, parting his thick red hair with his fingers. 'See, you can feel them, here.'

There were two scabs on his white scalp, the skin around them reddened and still slightly swollen. I didn't want to touch them but he insisted. 'He hit hard,' I said. 'It must have hurt. A lot of blood too, from head wounds. What happened then?'

He turned back towards the moat, leaning forward, elbows on knees, holding his ale in both hands. I had the impression he was settling in to an account he enjoyed giving. 'Blood everywhere. I couldn't see at first. Feared for my life. Wouldn't you? Didn't know what was going on or when he would stop and couldn't do anything because there was no room to move. The bench he was lying on was right behind me, see, in the bay window, with my chair almost right up against it and the others sitting at either end of the table so I couldn't get out forwards or sideways. I couldn't even get to my feet at first because I couldn't straighten my legs. When I did I could only half turn and lift my arm, my right arm, to ward off his blows. Like this, see?' He got to his feet in a half-crouch, his arm raised and the upper part of his body turned towards me.

I nodded and he sat again. 'I could see he was going to keep pommelling me and I grabbed his wrist and pushed it back. He was still coming at me with the blade pointing at him now. It went into his eye, just above it. I didn't realise it had gone in at first because his fist and mine were in the way and there was all this blood pouring down my face. Then he cried out and stopped, just stood where he was for a moment. Then went down on his knees with me still holding his wrist and the knife came out and there was blood spurting down his face too. I let go and he dropped the knife and put his hands to his face, cursing and swearing. Then he shut up and just subsided down onto his side, quite slowly. Half under the bench, he was.' Frizer turned to me again, his eyes wide with challenge. 'Good riddance, I say. Maybe he was your friend, but it served the bugger right.'

I remembered what Christopher said after the death of William Bradley in the Hog Lane affray. A whole world dies when a man dies, he said. What a world died with Christopher. Yet death is not an event, he also said. Nothing happens, just a ceasing. Nothing to fear, therefore, and nothing to come. Well, he would know now whether that was right. Or rather, if he knew anything at all he would know he was wrong.

The carp turned in the moat, great fat creatures, their fins breaking the surface. To keep Frizer talking I had to appear sympathetic. 'He had a temper, no doubt about it. He was known for it.'

'Ever up for a fight, was Kit. Little tyke. He won't be fighting now, that's for sure. Unless with the Devil.'

'He was always fighting the Devil. What provoked it this time? Why did he attack you?'

He kicked a stone into the water and sat watching the ripples. 'Fourpence, that's all. Wouldn't believe it, would you? Fourpence.'

'The reckoning?'

'Whose share was what. We argued over it. Robert – Robert Poley – said we should split it between the four of us, the taking of the room and the victuals. Kit said he'd pay his share of the victuals but not the room because he'd had nothing to do with it, which was true in a way. Robert had taken the room to meet me and Nicholas Skeres, for business. Kit came along because he had to report to the Council at Greenwich on these Ralegh matters, which was just down the road, and also he had some – some business ideas of his own. So I said do your Council stuff early and come and join us. Which is what he did. So he argued he only owed for his share of the victuals. Said it really angry, as if we'd been arguing about it, which we hadn't. He had a point, I doubt Robert would have pushed it. Anyway, knowing what a mean bugger he always was, I said over my shoulder that he was so tight we could hear his arse squeak. Next thing I knew he was bashing me about the head. I only meant in jest, really. Though he was tight. It was all over before it started, so far as I was concerned. Just shows, you never know.'

There was no hint of remorse in his tone or expression, though his last few words sounded thoughtful.

'So he contributed to the business of the meeting, then? He wasn't just there for food and drink?'

'He did, he did. That's why Poley said equal shares for all because Kit would have shared the proceeds if – you know, if it had all gone ahead.'

'If what had gone ahead?'

I had tried to sound as if I wasn't greatly interested but he was immediately defensive. 'Nothing much, future plans, that's all.'

'Ten in the morning until six in the evening is a long time to discuss nothing much.'

'Not where property's concerned. Always complicated, property matters. And Widow Bull does a good spread. Looks after her gentlemen. Good food and good drink. Makes it hard to leave.' He turned to me with a grin.

'Property matters' could mean everything or nothing, from great estates to bundles of kindling. It came out in court later that Frizer and Skeres were at that time plucking the feathers of a naive young heir, Drew Woodleff. They lent him money in return for a bond repayable by sale of commodities that they controlled and which would never make anything like the sum owing, leaving him potentially forfeiting his property. That was their usual game.

But it was very unlikely that this was what they met to discuss that day. Small beer for Poley, who sought to benefit from great affairs of state, while Christopher, I hope and still believe, would disdain such cozenage, even as cover for meeting. When he was freed from gaol following the Bradley affray he spoke of the many victims of such deceits he had met there, all imprisoned for debt as I am now. Some went mad or hanged themselves with the new moon. I can understand that.

On the other hand, Christopher admitted that it was in gaol that he learned about coining. That might have been what they were discussing, a grand coining fraud overseas as alleged in the Flushing business. Christopher could plausibly have contributed his knowledge and it would have been good reason to get himself into the meeting. But it was clear I wasn't going to get much more out of Frizer that day. The rack would doubtless have yielded an answer but from what Sir Robert had said there was no question of official proceedings.

My talk with Frizer was ended by Sir Thomas's return from hunting, so I had no chance to smoke out anything about what Poley was up to. He probably wouldn't have told me, anyway, even if he knew. I got in a mention of the Earl of Essex, asking if Skeres was still in his service. Frizer shrugged. 'Far as I know.'

'Fortunate for him.'

'Long as it lasts.'

Sir Thomas greeted me kindly and invited me to stay, though he was clearly going to be busy entertaining his huntsmen and would have no time for private discussion. I gave him the letters I carried and asked whether I might visit him again to discuss Christopher and his poetry. 'Most certainly,' he said earnestly, gripping my hand. 'He is much missed here. I – myself – I miss him badly.'

Although we spoke again later that day we did not discuss Christopher. Nor did I question Frizer any further. As for Sir Robert's worry about Poley and Frizer being poached by Essex, I doubted it from the first. But it was not in my interest to say so until I had completed and been paid for my investigation. It was not that I thought the Earl of Essex too honourable to plot in this manner, nor because I doubted that he would recruit Poley to his cause if he could. No, it was because I thought him incapable.

The whole thing was too subtle for him. If he had been capable of such subtlety he would not have gone about town rejoicing openly when Ralegh was disgraced for marrying Elizabeth Throgmorton, one of the Queen's ladies-in-waiting, without permission. The Queen banned them both from Court and they had to remove themselves to Devon. By rejoicing so openly Essex made himself look stupid. I expect, sir, that you know the story of his bursting in upon the Queen while she was dressing, an unforgiveable presumption? And how afterwards he mocked her aged appearance before his courtiers? That showed him to be as ill-mannered as he was crass. It is also said that in exasperation he once turned his back on her at Court, his hand on the hilt of his sword. That alone was enough for his death warrant, without his later allowing his supporters to shout against the Queen in the streets and briefly even to take up arms. He thought he had the woman in the palm of his hand, but he reckoned not with the monarch. No, sir, this was not a man who could plot and scheme as Robert Cecil – who certainly could – feared.

Yes, it is true that there were some who said after the event that Ralegh himself contrived Christopher's death for fear that he might tell the Council of Ralegh's own free-thinking and heresies. But that was even greater nonsense, to my mind. I have been at the heart of many secrets and plots, as you know, great plots with great consequences. I know how hard it is to bring off a plot successfully, how many have to be involved and how difficult are timing and coordination. It is fantastical to think that Ralegh could have engineered such a thing from Devonshire, even had he wanted to. He was a leader and a philosopher, maybe a heretic, but he was no plotter. What of all the others who were involved with him? Would he have had to murder them too when they were investigated?

I next saw Nicholas Skeres. Frizer was a rough diamond but with him you at least knew what you were getting. With Skeres you never knew where he stood because he was forever shifting according to where he thought you stood. He was a man without qualities, a chameleon who took on the shapes and colours of whomever he was with but whose one consistency was the relentless pursuit of his own advantage. He was like Poley but shallower and more obvious, lacking Poley's charm. He was lucky to survive Essex's eventual downfall, though as I think I've said already he spent much of the rest of his life in prison for his cozening.

Since we had no natural way of meeting – because of the way my earlier work for Lord Essex had ended I was reluctant to remind him or his circle of my existence – it took time to devise an encounter. Eventually I contrived to run into him on the street after one of his court appearances. I feigned delight and surprise, which should have alerted him since we were never close. He seemed preoccupied and distracted and I took advantage of his state to offer him sustenance in an inn. He was never one to refuse free fodder.

For a while we discussed mutual acquaintances and the progress of the case against him, which of course I agreed was monstrously unjust and unreasonable. I compared it with a former and equally monstrous case against both him and Frizer which I knew about. Having mentioned Frizer, I was then able to ask after him.

'He does well enough for himself,' he said with a hint of resentment. 'He manages properties for Thomas Walsingham and his wife. He is trusted with the rents.' He rubbed his forrid with the back of his hand, a regular habit.

More than you would be, I thought. 'He did well to come out of the Kit Marlowe affair with no stain upon him.'

His pale blue eyes looked out at me from beneath his hand. 'He deserved to, it was not his fault. Marlowe fell upon him of a sudden.'

'Why? What provoked it?'

'The reckoning. They argued about the reckoning.'

'Is that all? Nothing else?'

'It was enough. Marlowe was close with money.'

'I had heard there was something else, some disagreement.'

He shrugged. 'They goaded each other. They always did.'

'But Frizer had invited him that day, had he not?'

'So far as I know. I didn't know he would be there. They came from Scadbury where they stayed with Thomas Walsingham. I came from London.'

'What was it about, the meeting?'

Until that point he had answered carelessly, as if the whole episode was of little concern and he was weary of it. But now the vacancy of his pale eyes became a deliberate, sullen blankness. 'Property matters.'

'I didn't know Marlowe had an interest in property. He didn't own any, did he?'

'He could've if he hadn't lost his temper.'

'That was ever his fault.' We sat in silence. I sensed that he was about to leave, having had his fill. 'Of course, he was reporting to the Court at this time, wasn't he? An investigation into heresies?'

'Something like that.'

'He was associated with Sir Walter Ralegh, I heard.'

'Maybe.' He shrugged. 'There wasn't much blood. Considering it killed him, there wasn't much.'

'Frizer must've stabbed hard.'

'He didn't stab at all. He grabbed his arm and Marlowe's momentum carried him onto the knife.'

'The blade was pointing backwards at him, was it?'

'Couldn't see clearly from where I was. But it must've been because he was pommelling him. It was over so quickly, over before it started.'

'There was bad blood between them, wasn't there? Ingram and Marlowe?'

'They niggled each other, as I said. Marlowe especially. He had a way of getting under Ingram's skin. Walsingham kept the peace.'

'What was it that got under Marlowe's skin that day?'

'Didn't like hearing the truth about himself.'

'Which was?'

The blankness returned to his eyes. 'What d'you want to know for? He's dead. It was self-defence, no question about it, the law says. His own fault. What's your interest?'

'He was a friend, I liked him.'

'No one else misses him. Cocky bastard.' He yawned.

I offered more ale but he was tired, he said, had had enough talk for one day. We parted with the simulacrum of fellowship, never to meet again. That would have troubled neither of us, had we known it.

Robert Poley was another matter but I didn't have to seek him out: he came to me, knocking on the door of our house in Leadenhall Street one morning. It was my late father's house, Mary's being then let to another play-maker and poet who shared it with a doctor. Poley was smiling and breezy, an honest man of the world going cheerfully about his business. We sat at my table with ale, bread and cheese. He asked what I did to keep body and soul together. I had actually been doing a small piece of French deciphering for Sir Robert but couldn't talk about that so I talked about the family business I had inherited, the collection of duties on behalf of the custom house. It was flourishing although hard to keep track of it all, even with Mary's help. In the past my secret work had been a great distraction and I knew the business owed the Queen considerable sums going back to my father's time, but it was a problem to estimate them. With some of the money I had enlarged my lands in Yorkshire and Essex, intending to pay what I owed from the earnings, but that had not always proved possible. Also, I never had payment for my work for

218

Mr Secretary, only occasional favours, as was the custom then. It was a great favour that he had secured for me a pension from the Queen of 100 guineas a year for delivering Babington.

Poley broke his bread and cheese into little pieces – he had few teeth left – and asked how the collection of duties worked. He obviously had some scheme afoot, since I had never known him so amiable, but I knew better than to ask. If he wanted me to know he would tell me; if he didn't he would mislead me, no matter how I asked.

Eventually, he said, 'You must wonder why I ask these questions, Thomas.'

'You have your eye on a similar position for yourself?'

'No, but I wonder whether the money you collect could be put to better use, whether it could be made to work harder.'

'For me?'

'For us both.'

The scheme he outlined showed he was not above coney-catching provided the rewards were big enough. Not that he personally was involved in luring coneys into debt. That was done by what he called business associates, in other words Frizer and Skeres and others unknown. He sought funds to buy the lands and houses of victims forced to sell at knock-down prices in order to relieve the debts he had led them into. It was not quite usury so far as the law was concerned for they were not charged interest, which had a legal limit of 10 per cent. Rather, in return for a promissory note they were offered whatever sum they needed in the form of a commodity. In the case of the young man Woodleff, whom Frizer and Skeres were skinning, the commodity was guns or great iron pieces which he was told he could then sell to raise the money to pay his debt. When he came to sell, however, he would find no buyers except those who had led him into debt. They would offer a much lower price and then demand repayment in full of the promissory note. Unable to find this, his entire property would be forfeit. His kindly creditors would then offer to bail him out at a fraction of its value.

'We have a long list of properties,' Poley explained, 'which we can buy cheap and sell dear, sharing the proceeds. But we need more money than we have in order to buy even at our cheap rate. The duties you collect could be used to buy them before you pass them on to the Crown. Then we sell them, repay you and you pass on your duties and keep your share of the profit. You gain and the Queen loses nothing.'

That was very like what I was trying to do anyway, albeit on my own behalf and without luring foolish young men into debt. And I was becoming well aware of the drawbacks, of the difficulty of selling or letting for the sums I had anticipated or in the time permitted. I anticipated trouble with Lord Burghley, the Lord Treasurer, about this so it was not hard to say no to Poley.

But I didn't say no straight away. I tried to sound as if I were considering it. 'Is this what you were planning with Kit Marlowe when he lost his temper with Frizer that day in Deptford?'

He shook his head, frowning. 'That was a Dutch scheme. Property scheme. Didn't come off. Could still, I suppose, but Marlowe had good contacts there, or said he had. Don't have any yourself, do you?'

'I don't, but I know he had a bit of trouble there not long before. I'm surprised he considered going back.'

'He wouldn't have had to. Coining he was done for, wasn't he? Nearly. That could be done here as well as there, so long as you've got the wherewithal and you grease the right palms for getting it over there.'

'So coining was what it was about, your meeting?'

Poley didn't like repeated direct questions. 'That and other matters.'

If he'd been on the rack I'd have asked much more but Robert Poley was never put anywhere near the rack himself, though he saw that a few were sent to it. 'I never thought Christopher Marlowe was serious about coining.'

'Don't know that he was, really. It was just a step towards alchemy for him.'

'Alchemy?'

'You know, turning base metal into gold. He was writing about it in one of his plays, he said, about a man who thought he'd found the secret. All bollocks, if you ask me, but he wanted to have a go, or find someone who could.'

'That wasn't why Frizer invited him along, surely?'

'He had to be in Greenwich anyway, to report the Court.'

That was a typical Poley answer, the truth but not the whole truth. But he had implicitly conceded that the invitation was

Frizer's. 'That was a funny business, that free-thinking investigation,' I continued. 'Where did it all come from?'

He shook his head again, this time grinning. 'You must know about that. You sit on the Dutch Church libel commission. You know very well where it came from.'

There was almost nothing that man didn't know. 'Not from us, not from the commission. We'd cleared him. Whoever did it quoted from his plays, true enough, but it wasn't him. But someone was pursuing him for free-thinking.' I paused to see if he volunteered anything. 'Is it someone after Ralegh? Could he be the real target? Has anyone from Essex's circle been sniffing around?'

He shrugged. 'No idea.'

'There's Skeres, of course. He's an Essex man, isn't he?'

'Likes to think he is. I wouldn't get too near Essex if I was him.'

Was his indifference natural or just a little too studied? He was so accustomed to dissembling that the act had become the man, the habit so ingrained that he concealed by habit even when there was nothing to hide. 'So how did it happen?'

'How did what happen?'

'Marlowe. The fight, the killing. How did it start?'

He looked, or affected to look, as if he were struggling to recall something from the distant past. 'Oh that, that business. Well, they were arguing, they'd been bickering all morning, rubbing each other up the wrong way. Never got on, those two, despite taking Walsingham's bread and living under his roof.'

'Yet Frizer had invited Marlowe to the meeting.'

'For his Dutch contacts, not to listen to all his guff about alchemy. I'd just come from Holland, I knew the possibilities. And then there was an argument about who paid what to Widow Bull. Marlowe didn't want to pay his full whack for the room and all because it was already set up without him. He just wanted to pay his share of the victuals. As he well should've, he'd drunk enough for all of us. He had a point, but him and Frizer were as mean as each other and this was just one more thing. Frizer called him a tight-arse and next thing we knew he had Frizer's dagger from his belt and was knocking him about the head with the pommel.'

'What about his own dagger?'

'He'd taken his sword and buckle off when we sat and put them in the corner with his belt. He was lying down, you see, on the bench at the side.'

'And Frizer's blade got pushed into Marlowe's eye?'

'So he says, Frizer. I didn't see it until after it happened. It was all so quick. They both fell against me, almost knocked me off my chair. Then Marlowe went down, taking Frizer with him, nearly. He was cursing and holding his face and there was blood running down the backs of his hands.'

'He died quick, then?'

'Pretty quick.'

He spoke more freely now, whether because he was describing something still vivid or because he was rehearsing an agreed account I couldn't say. The three accounts matched, as the coroner had found, but you'd expect that, whether true or false. 'Some say his death was planned,' I ventured.

His surprise looked genuine, although it would, of course, with Poley. 'Who says? Who by and for what?'

'Rumours, gossip, loose talk in taverns. Don't credit it myself but it's what people say.'

Poley shook his head. 'If anyone wanted Kit Marlowe dead there were easier ways of doing it than staging a fight you have to justify in court. A walk by the river after dark and a shove off the jetty would've done for him, the amount he'd drunk. Went for a piss and must have fell in, was all you'd need to say. I've known it done.'

I didn't doubt it.

I rode out to Scadbury again a few weeks after I had talked to Frizer there, bearing another contrived message from Sir Robert. I had high hopes that Thomas Walsingham might be more forthcoming than the others because he appreciated drama and poetry and had evidently been fond of Christopher. He might have known him more person-ally rather than merely as a possible business partner. And Christopher must have admired and felt something for him because his long poem *Hero and Leander*, although not pub-lished until about five years after his death, was dedicated to Thomas Walsingham. It is a very great poem, I understand.

He received me most cordially, entertaining me for the night as a great storm came on which would have made my journey home treacherous. After we had dined his wife retired and Thomas and I sat by the fire in the hall. Frizer, happily, was away in nearby Eltham on some business or other. I have heard he lives there still, a respectable family man, churchwarden and tax assessor. Other than myself, he is the only one still living who was involved in that business. Yet he, the man who killed Christopher, who felt his last breath and his blood hot on his hands, is not questioned about this matter. So why am I? Can you at least tell me that, sir?

Ah, is that so? You have? His mind wanders. Thought you were the King, did he? And has no memory of Christopher? Or so he says. Well, it comes to us all if we live long enough.

Back to Thomas Walsingham, yes. He wished he had known Christopher better, he said. Every day he wished that. Until Christopher was gone he did not realise how often he thought of him, how frequently his words came into his head, how much more he would have asked him. I told him I felt the same. As we spoke his brown eyes became soft and melancholy and his beard took on a reddish tinge in the firelight. 'You are familiar with his verses?'

'No, to my sorrow, I am not.'

'You should be.'

'How did Frizer kill him?'

He sighed. 'They argued, I understand, and Christopher attacked him. They were never friends, always sparks between them. Christopher was drunk, they told me. I can believe that. He was becoming too fond of his drink and he was prone to – to passions, drunk or sober. Did you find that? Did you know him in his passion?'

'I knew him for a fighter when roused.'

He looked at me as if expecting me to go on, then turned back to the fire. 'I was more than sad when I heard. I had hoped that we – he and I – but I cannot blame Ingram. It was not his fault. And Christopher was fiery in his passions.'

'There was nothing behind his death? No one who wanted him dead or quietened?'

'Why should anyone want that? He was no threat to anyone.' He continued staring into the fire, then added quietly, 'There was some jealousy between them, I suppose. Him and Ingram.'

'Jealousy of what?'

'Personal, merely personal.'

I never did discover what he meant. I asked about Ralegh and free-thinking and Christopher's work for us, which Thomas knew all about, but neither of us could think of any plausible plot or motive for a conspiracy to kill him. I mentioned Essex, too, saying that Skeres had become a servant of Essex. Had Frizer?

Thomas shook his head. 'Ingram is not a political animal. He is a practical down-to-earth man. Any talk of Court affairs frightens him. It's the only thing that does, I think.'

'And Poley? He is a very political animal.'

'And a very cautious one. That is how he survives. He serves Robert Cecil, does he not? He wouldn't jump from that ship unless he knew it was sinking. Which it plainly isn't, from what I see. Father and son have their hands on the tiller. The Queen heeds them, not Essex, not Ralegh, nor anyone else.'

I mentioned tavern rumours to the effect that Christopher's death might have been intended or willed by free-thinkers around Ralegh in order to protect themselves. He was as unpersuaded as I was.

'It doesn't make any sense. Ralegh is keeping his head down in Devon. If anyone worried about what Christopher might say they'd get him to flee abroad. As he could have done himself if he worried about anything. Instead, he was content – more than content, happy – to stay here writing his verse and reporting to the Council as required. Anyway, if you wanted to murder someone you wouldn't do it like that, would you? Too complicated.'

It is often thus, I find, with conspiracy theories: the more you probe them, the emptier they become. I have spent much of my life amid real conspiracies, as you know, sir, and as I have said already I know how complicated, expensive, hard to contrive and few they are. Men love to see them everywhere, overcoming all objections by widening the circle of conspiracy so that in time half the world is party to it and it is impossible we should not all know of it.

The last person I spoke to was Eleanor Bull. I rode to her house in Deptford on my way back from Scadbury, following the route that Christopher would have taken on his last journey. The house was easily found, a fine building of three storeys on the Strand, set back from the street with a large garden to the rear. A maid wearing a clean white apron answered my knock and civilly bade me wait. She left the door ajar and I heard her tell her mistress there was a gentleman asking for her. She returned to say that Mrs Bull sent her respects but she was fully booked. I asked that she return to Mrs Bull and say that I came to see her in connection with the matter that had brought the coroner to her house earlier in the summer. After another muttered conversation within, I was bidden enter.

Mrs Bull was a well-dressed lady of ample girth with a round, red, wrinkled face. She was stiff with me at first, perhaps suspecting that I was a court official with some question or complaint. But when I told her I was a friend of the late Christopher Marlowe and that I had been asked by his family to establish the circumstances of his death and burial, and to retrieve any goods or possessions he might have left behind, she began to relax.

'He left nothing here apart from his belt with his sword and knife and they disappeared when his body was taken. Whether the coroner's men had them or Mr Poley, I know not.'

'It was Mr Poley who made the booking, I believe?'

'One of my regular gentlemen, Mr Poley.' She nodded and smiled. 'Whenever he comes from abroad. Such a gentleman.'

'And the others, were they regulars?'

'Off and on, they come to meet and drink and talk. And sometimes other gentlemen. Mr Marlowe, poor soul, I'd not seen before, but he was very nice, very polite. He drank well. They all did, except Mr Poley. He is always moderate in his drinking.'

'Was Mr Marlowe drunk that day?'

Her cheeks wobbled as she shook her head. 'That I couldn't say, sir. He may have been. They had plenty to drink, as I said, but who had what I know not. After they had eaten I left them to themselves in their room and saw nothing of them until – until the rumpus.'

'What occasioned it?'

'An argument, they said. Mr Poley told me at the time it was about the reckoning and the coroner said so too, afterwards. We down here knew nothing of it until we heard raised voices – you could hear them from the kitchen – and then a stumbling about and thumping and banging and a shout and then silence. A long silence. And then Mr Poley came out and called downstairs for cloths and bandages, and to come quick.'

She obligingly showed me the room. It was on the first floor at the back, overlooking the garden and beyond it the river. A fine room with fresh panelling and a bay window with a window seat stretching the width of it. There was a table across the width of the bay with four chairs. Mrs Bull understood that Christopher had been lying on the window seat, with Frizer on the chair with his back to him and the other two on chairs at the ends of the table. Neither Christopher nor Frizer could have got out into the room without moving the table, or the others moving their chairs.

'They were playing at cards,' she said. 'There was money involved in that too. Maybe they argued about the winnings as well as my reckoning. The cards were all a mess on the table when I came in and Mr Frizer's chair was overturned and the table pushed out at an angle. Mr Marlowe was lying here' – she pointed to the floor between the table and the window seat – 'with his mouth open and a horrid gash in his eye, or near as made no difference, God bless his soul. There was blood on the floor and some on the table and one of the other gentlemen, Mr Frizer it was, was standing there with blood pouring from the top of his head, all down his face. And the cards were all messed up, as I said.'

I stared at the spot where he died as if to read something in it. But silence is all we learn from death. He was buried two days after, she told me, in St Nicholas's church, in a grave just beyond the north wall of the tower. The graveyard was almost full and soon would be if the plague reached them from London, God forbid. The only mourner apart from herself was Sir Thomas Walsingham. He paid for the burial, she said. There was talk of a memorial stone.

'Such a kind man, Sir Thomas. A real gentleman. He is acquainted with the Lord Burghley to whom I am distantly related. I have been at Court, sir, when Mr Bull was alive.'

'So I have heard.'

She swelled with pride. 'I keep my house for gentlemen, only for gentlemen. I worried that what had happened to Mr Marlowe would bring us ill repute, as if I kept a bawdy house, but Sir Thomas was kind enough to return with me here for refreshment so that all could see we are respectable.'

'Did he say anything about Mr Marlowe?'

'He shed a tear or two and said a great voice was silenced. I hadn't known Mr Marlowe was a poet. He came from Canterbury, Sir Thomas said, and still has family there. I don't know who told them what happened.'

I called at the church afterwards. There were four fresh

graves outside the north wall, none marked. Three were very fresh, days old. Perhaps the plague had already reached Deptford. The fourth must have been his, the ground already slightly sunken. I stood by it and said a prayer for he who would have scorned such intercession. I suspect my prayer was as much for my own failing faith as to save him.

I thought of Christopher's family as I rode back to London that day, prompted by Mrs Bull's remark. He had never mentioned them, except to say his origins were humble. How many were there, how would news have reached Canterbury, who would have told them? And how long after? Was it possible that even now they did not know? I could have journeyed to see them but it would have been a melancholy business and I had had enough of melancholy. Also, I had tasks to perform, money to earn. Lives are like raindrops, a moment in the light and they are gone, but life itself goes on.

'Was he a lost soul?' I had asked Sir Thomas as I sat in the saddle that morning.

'A bright star doomed by his own will,' he said. 'I pray he repents and is spared Hell.'

I now know that Christopher wrote about Hell but I do not believe he feared it. Or believed in it. What troubled him, troubled and fascinated him, was the prospect of nothingness, nothingness everlasting, absence eternal. He infected me with it and it troubles me still, even in this cell where I would rather live and feel the cold and damp than die and feel nothing.

And yet, and yet. There was an honesty about Christopher,

about his contempt for pretence and his thirst for truth even where no truth is to be found. Thinking of him gives me – not hope, exactly – but a sense that if there is anything beyond us, we must endure its absence before we find it.

Chapter Twelve

Before you go, sir, may I beg a favour? May I beg that in submitting these my humble recollections you remind His Majesty of my pension of 100 guineas a year, given me by Queen Elizabeth but taken away to pay off my debts to the Crown after she died? I sorely miss it and if His Majesty should see fit to restore it in return for my help in this matter and for any other help His Majesty requires, I should be eternally grateful.

I confess I misappropriated Crown funds and am grossly indebted. I do not deny it. Unlike matters of state I had to do with, I managed my own affairs unwisely. I was both too careless with money and too grasping of it. I suffered Queen Elizabeth's tempestuous displeasure and, with Mr Secretary no longer at Court to speak for me, became all too familiar with the Marshalsea and Fleet gaols, later with the Gatehouse and even the Tower itself. I have endured a quarter of a century of intermittent incarcerations and now you find me still here, in the King's Bench prison. I am told the law should not permit my close confinement any longer yet here I am, giving you this account for His Majesty. When not so employed I am still asked to decipher, despite failing sight, lack of my records and an uncertain mind. Were it not for my good wife Mary obtaining some relief from the late Sir Robert Cecil, and keeping up my correspondence, and seeing to our properties, and furthering our Dutch scheme for turning iron into steel, I do believe I should have starved or wasted with disease like so many of the wretches around me. If it should please His Majesty to release me, I should be truly, humbly grateful.

True, sir, true, I have been released before and each time eventually returned. As I have mentioned, I was released to help with the investigation into the men who plotted to murder all His Majesty's government in parliament. They prepared a great explosion with barrels of powder beneath the chamber. The records will show that I was most useful to William Waad in his interrogations. Yet even after that I was returned to the Tower for corresponding with an acquaintance abroad I had known for many years who was familiar with the plot and from whom I derived good intelligence about it. That was the sole purpose of my correspondence but I was treated as a traitor.

Even now I might be of more help to His Majesty if only I could know why His Majesty wants to know about Christopher Marlowe. I could shape my account to his desires instead of telling you much you may not need to know.

Is it for his plays? I know little of them and suspect they are not often performed now.

Is it for the work he did for Mr Secretary, for his part in bringing the King's mother to trial?

Is it for his verses? I understand the King has a fondness for verses.

Is it for his free-thinking, then, his association with Sir Walter Ralegh? I confess that is what I have all along thought it must be. I know Ralegh was no favourite of the King's and is anyway now long parted from his head.

Or is it that tavern talk that Christopher was victim of a conspiracy, that he was murdered, has reached the King at last? I did not believe it at the time and do not now. Even when the events were fresh none could say why or by whom his death was desired, and certainly none has since. I counsel His Majesty not to heed such talk. Why anyway should he be interested? I have told you all I know, or think I know, but if you could please tell me why, just one word, I could perhaps tell more.

A sodomite? Was Christopher a sodomite? Is that all, sir? His Majesty wants to know whether Christopher Marlowe was killed for being a sodomite?

Well, truly, I never knew him for one. I never thought of it. I told you what Thomas Kyd, when racked, said about Christopher and tobacco and boys. But that is the kind of thing Christopher would say. He liked to provoke. I never knew him go with a boy or a man. Or a woman, come to that.

And if he had, why should he have been killed for it when he could have been brought to law? If he had been brought to law for blasphemy, heresy and free-thinking, his accusers would surely have added unnatural practices if they had evidence? But if it is the King's thinking that Christopher was killed to stop him talking, then please beg His Majesty's mercy and say I can help no more, alas.

And yet, and yet. I have heard that his plays touch upon love between men. And if it is also true, as I have also heard that the King himself has favourites, could it be that—?

Of course, sir, of course. I have uttered no such thing, nor would I.

But please remember, sir, that I began this account by saying I could not promise to decipher Christopher Marlowe for you. The Devil alone knoweth the heart of man, a learned judge once wrote.

What I can say is that a man is more than his proclivities. Christopher had hot blood and a fearless mind. He walked where the rest of us fear to tread and he dissolved my faith in the life to come. Yet he sought not to destroy, but to be true. His bequest to me was honest doubt. That is what I believe is important about him, more than his plays or his verses, of which I know sadly little. His life showed that the courage to be honest is the best exemplar of whatever life might be to come. If there is one. And if there is no life to come, only nothingness, then being honest about that and living fully in the face of nothing is an even greater virtue, the very best we can do. And that surely is deserving of something.

POSTSCRIPT

Extract from letter dated 16 February 1626 from Sir Edward Conway, Gent., to the Duke of Buckingham, counsellor to King James I and King Charles I.

... Further to which, Your Grace will be familiar with the desire of His late Majesty, King James of blessed memory, to know the circumstances of the death of the poet Christopher Marlowe in 1593 during the reign of Queen Elizabeth. Although I know not whether King Charles hath inherited his father's interest, nonetheless I humbly submit the last of my reports on this matter. It is the account given me by Thomas Phelippes, the famed man of ciphers who dwelt in the world of those who witnessed the death of the poet, and who did know them all. I questioned him in the King's Bench prison where, at Your Grace's order, he was granted his own more commodious cell and adequate supplies. The account is in his words, so far as I could render them.

Phelippes spoke not knowing the reason for King

James's interest until near the end of my questioning
when I described it in as few words as Your Grace was
pleased to use with me, at the behest of the King. Your
Grace having been intimate with King James's desires
in this matter, I take the liberty of assuming that Your
Grace has a like intimacy now with King Charles which
will guide Your Grace in deciding whether to show this
report to His Majesty. There is much in it to offend any
good Christian and I beg Your Grace please to assure His
Majesty that not a word of what Thomas Phelippes said
shall be bruited abroad. Besides, the man is dead.

It was thanks to Your Grace's intervention that
Phelippes's last months in prison were considerably
eased. There were divers reasons why he spent his old
age in and out – indeed, more in than out – of gaol. He
was much troubled by litigation concerning an estate he
bought at Kirkby Misperton in Yorkshire, his feud with
Sir Anthony Ashley lasted above fifteen years and an old
quarrel between him and one Tyttyn saw him returned
to gaol some years ago. For all his genius with number
and cipher, and his skill as an intelligencer, he was not
apt at handling his own affairs. His earlier years in
confinement arose from his mishandling of his customs
dues, as you may see from his account. He earned
thereby the wrath of Queen Elizabeth herself and the ill
opinion of Lord Burlegh.

Further, when certain treasonous gentlemen
attempted to murder King James and his ministers in

Parliament in 1605 he was released from prison to help
catch the plotters, as he tells us. But afterwards he was
confined forthwith to the Tower for more than four
years. This was because of his correspondence with
Hugh Owen, one of the Duke of Parma's intelligencers
in Brussels who was aiding the Spanish cause and
whose evil doings were known to King James. Phelippes
protested that he had maintained this correspondence
since the old Queen's time but always using other
names. At different times and with various men he was
known as Peter Halins, John Morice, Henry Willsdon
or John Wystand, and no doubt he used others too. His
purpose was to draw out Owen, who thought he was
dealing with sympathisers. Nobody, not even Sir Robert
Cecil himself, could determine the truth of this and he
was eventually freed. But by then prison had damaged
him in body and mind. I examined his seized papers
myself, after questioning him, and although I could
reach no firm conclusion I believe his intention was as he
described. He was no traitor.

He fell into trouble again more recently when the
Venetian ambassador sent to him to test the Venetian
ciphers. They thought him unequalled in deciphering,
as he indeed he was, but this time their ciphers defeated
him, a defeat he attributed to his near-blindness and
his long disuse of the Italian language. Also, he was
denied access in prison to his records, in absence of
which he revealed the cipher key to another prisoner

sent to read for him. The ambassador protested and it was determined he should remain in prison, despite the ambassador later saying he had dealt sincerely with them and should have been paid for his services. He did similar work for us, of course, but never was he paid.

Following my questioning of him, as Your Grace will know from previous correspondence, I petitioned for his release on the ground that the laws did not allow his close confinement any longer. My efforts carried little weight but when Your Grace saw fit to endorse the petition it was graciously granted by His Majesty, though not until this year. It is with sadness that I confess I do not yet know whether he lived to be released into the arms of his good wife. To be sure, if he was released, he did not live long. His widow, Mary, is a worthy woman who for many years worked hard to sustain their affairs. She is a loyal subject, of good faith, and now she has none to support her. Your Grace will I hope permit me to petition for a small pension for her in hopes that His Majesty, counselled by Your Grace, will look upon it with favour. His faults notwithstanding, Thomas Phelippes did the state some service.

I am, Sir, Your Obedient servant . . .

ABOUT THE AUTHOR

Alan Judd is the multiple award-winning author of fifteen novels, three of which have been filmed. He has also written two major biographies, *Ford Madox Ford* and *The Quest for C*, the authorized biography of the founder of MI6. Before becoming a full-time writer, he served in the Army and the Foreign Office and was subsequently a columnist for the *Daily Telegraph* and the *Spectator*. He currently writes the motoring column for the *Oldie*.